BEAUTY AND THE BLACKSMITH

By Tessa Dare

Beauty and the Blacksmith
The Scandalous, Dissolute, No-Good Mr. Wright
A Lady by Midnight
A Week to Be Wicked
A Night to Surrender
Three Nights with a Scoundrel
Twice Tempted by a Rogue
One Dance with a Duke
A Lady of Persuasion
Surrender of a Siren
Goddess of the Hunt

Coming Soon
Any Duchess Will Do

BEAUTY AND
THE BLACKSMITH

A Spindle Cove Novella

TESSA DARE

AVONIMPULSE
An Imprint of HarperCollinsPublishers

Excerpt from *Any Duchess Will Do* copyright © 2013 by Eve Ortega.

BEAUTY AND THE BLACKSMITH. Copyright © 2013 by Eve Ortega. All rights reserved under International and Pan-American Copyright Conventions. By payment of the required fees, you have been granted the nonexclusive, nontransferable right to access and read the text of this e-book on screen. No part of this text may be reproduced, transmitted, decompiled, reverse-engineered, or stored in or introduced into any information storage and retrieval system, in any form or by any means, whether electronic or mechanical, now known or hereinafter invented, without the express written permission of HarperCollins e-books.

EPub Edition MAY 2013 ISBN: 9780062238849
Print Edition ISBN: 9780062238856

Beauty and the Blacksmith

CHAPTER 1

Goodness. Just look at it. Thick as my ankle.

Diana Highwood took her glove and worked it like a fan, chasing the flush from her throat. She was a gentlewoman, born and raised in genteel comfort, if not opulent luxury. From an early age, she'd been marked as the hope of the family. Destined, her mother vowed, to catch a nobleman's eye.

But here, in the smithy with Aaron Dawes, all her delicate breeding disintegrated.

How could she help staring? The man had wrists as thick as her *ankle*.

As always, he wore his sleeves rolled to the elbow, exposing forearms roped with muscle. He pumped the bellows, commanding the flames to dance.

Broad shoulders stretched his homespun shirt, and a leather apron hung low on his hips. As he removed the glowing bit of metal from the fire and placed it on his anvil, his open collar gaped.

Diana averted her gaze—but not fast enough. She caught a moment's glimpse of pure, superheated virility. Sculpted chest muscles, bronzed skin, dark hair . . .

"Behave yourself," he said.

The words startled her breathless.

He knows. He knows. He's realized that refined, perfect, gently bred Miss Highwood comes to the smithy to gawp at his brute manliness. Behave yourself, indeed.

She felt ridiculous. Ashamed. Exposed.

And then—suddenly—relieved.

He wasn't speaking to her. He was speaking to his work.

"That's it." Perspiration glistened on his brow. With a steady hand and a low, rich baritone, he finessed the broken clasp. "Be good for me now."

Diana turned her gaze downward, focusing on the floor. Neatly swept and fitted stones paved her half of the smithy, where visitors waited for their work. The ground around the forge was packed with black, smudgy cinders. And the border between the two could not have been more stark, or more meaningful.

Here was the division between customer and smith. The line between the world of a gentlewoman and a working man's domain.

"There we are," he said. "That's the way."

Oh, goodness. She could look away from his thick forearms and his muscled chest. But that *voice.*

She gave herself a brisk shake. Time to put a stop to this silliness. She was a grown woman, turning four-and-twenty this year. It was surely no sin to admire Mr. Dawes. He was an admirable man. However, she ought to concentrate on the many reasons that had nothing to do with carnality.

The Highwoods had come to this seaside village for Diana's health, but she'd come to think of Spindle Cove as home. During their stay, she'd learned a great deal about rural life. She knew a good village smith was indispensable. He shoed the farmers' draft horses, and he mended the oarlocks on the fishermen's boats. When neighbors were ailing, he pulled teeth and set broken bones. The nails struck on his anvil held the whole village together.

This forge was the glowing, iron heart of Spindle Cove, and Aaron Dawes was its pulse. Strong. Steady. Vital.

She watched him striking off beats with his hammer. *Clang. Clang. Clang.*

Now her eyes were fused to that forearm again.

"This weather," she said, trying to change the subject. "It's been a dreadful March, hasn't it?"

He grunted in agreement. "Near a fortnight now without sun."

He plunged the heated metal into a waiting bucket. A cloud of steam rose and filled the smithy, curling the short hairs at the nape of her neck.

"That should do," he said, examining the cooled clasp of her necklace. He polished it with a scrap of cloth. "Let's hope it lasts this time."

Diana gave him a nervous smile. "I do seem to have bad luck with it, don't I?"

"This is the third time it's broken this year, by my count. You must think my craftsmanship is faulty."

"No," she hastened to assure him. "Not at all. You do very good work, Mr. Dawes. I'm just careless, that's all."

"Careless? You?" His gaze locked with hers from across the smithy, dark and intense.

She caught him looking at her like this sometimes. In church, around the village. She didn't know what to make of her reaction, but she couldn't deny it was a thrilling sort of confusion.

He mopped his brow and neck with a damp cloth, then wiped his hands clean. "It's a curious thing, Miss Highwood. You don't strike me as the clumsy sort."

She shifted on her seat, uneasy.

"And of all things," he said, "I'd think you'd be careful with this."

She watched as he threaded the tiny vial back on its chain. In the vial was a tincture of shrubby horsetail. She kept a dose with her at all times, in case of a breathing crisis.

"You're right." Despite her accelerating pulse, she forced an easy smile. "I should be more cautious. I will be, in the future."

He looked up at her. "Are you well?"

"Quite."

"You look flushed."

"Oh. Er . . ."

He walked behind her and placed the chain about her neck, standing close to do the clasp. If she'd been flushed already, now she was enflamed. It was as though he'd soaked all the heat up from the fire, and now he gave it to her. Soothing and melting all her knotted places. Like the heated brick she took to bed when she had her courses.

Oh, Lord. The last thing she needed right now was

thoughts of bed. Much less this big, solid brick of masculinity sharing it.

"Still don't know how you managed to smash it like that," he said.

By slamming it in a drawer. And finishing the deed with a rock.

"I don't know, either," she prevaricated. Her heart thumped wildly in her chest.

"I could almost believe someone did it on purpose. I know accidents happen. But they don't usually happen the same way twice."

As he fastened the necklace, his fingertips brushed her neck.

Diana sucked in her breath. She wanted to pretend the touch was an accident. As he'd said, accidents happen.

But they didn't happen the same way twice.

He caressed her neck a second time, his roughened thumb sliding down the soft skin at her nape.

"Why are you here?" he asked.

She couldn't answer. She couldn't move, couldn't think.

"I wonder about it. Why you come so often. Why every metal latch and clasp and rivet you possess seems to need mending of late." His voice grew deeper, almost dreamy. "I've told myself you're just bored with this village. With this weather, there's little else to do."

He circled her, running his finger beneath that chain. Branding her with a necklace of his touch.

"Other times"—she caught a wry note in his voice—"I decide you've been sent by the devil to torment me for my sins."

He came to stand before her, holding that vial that dangled from her necklace. He pulled gently, and she swayed toward him. Just an inch.

"And then sometimes I think maybe . . . just maybe . . . you're hoping for something to happen. Something like this."

She swallowed hard, staring straight into the notch above his sternum. That shamelessly sensual crossroads of bone and muscle and sinew and skin.

The heat of him swamped her. She felt . . . It was so very odd, but she felt *ticklish*. As though every inch of her was exquisitely attuned, anticipating his touch.

Perhaps he was right.

Perhaps she had been wanting this.

He released her necklace. "Well?"

She gathered her courage and looked up at him. Outside of social calls and dinner parties, Diana had little experience with men. But if there was one thing her genteel upbringing had taught her, it was how to read an invitation.

If she gave Mr. Dawes the slightest encouragement . . .

Oh, heavens. He would kiss her. Those strong, sensual lips would be on hers, and his powerful arms would hold her tight, and there would be no taking the moment back. She would leave with a changed understanding of herself and smears of soot on her best blue frock. In the eyes of the world, she'd be soiled.

Dirty.

"I should go." The words erupted from her throat, like a geyser of panic. "I should go."

He nodded and stepped back at once. "You should go."

She hopped down from the stool and reached for her

cloak. The cloak didn't seem as eager to leave as she was. She wrestled with it, cursing the tangled laces.

"I'm not sure the smithy's the safest place for you, Miss Highwood." His manner was easy as he returned to the forge and pumped the bellows. "Lots of smoke and steam. Sparks have a tendency to fly."

"Perhaps you're right."

"Next time you have something what needs mending, just send it over with one of the rooming house maids."

"I'll do that." She made a desperate grab for the door, pulling it open. "Good day, Mr. Dawes."

"Good day, Miss Highwood."

She made it a respectable distance down the lane before stopping to press her hand to her chest. Closing her eyes, she inhaled a deep, steady breath.

Oh, Lord. What a fool she was.

Damn. Aaron felt like an idiot.

No, no. *Idiot* was too kind a word. Idiots were innocent of their mistakes. Aaron knew better. He was a coarse, mutton-brained lout.

What the devil had he been thinking? He didn't know what had made him do it. Only that she'd been wearing that china-blue frock with lacy edges—the one that made him want to carry her into a field of wildflowers, lay her down like a picnic blanket, and feast.

Perhaps it was best this way. She wouldn't come around to tempt him again—that much was certain.

Too much of the day remained, and he was too restless for

leisure. Lacking an urgent project, he pulled out some thin iron stock and decided to bang out nails. A smith could never have too many nails.

Again and again, he heated the rod to a glowing yellow, braced it on his anvil, and pounded one end to a tapered point. With an ease born of years of practice, he severed the length in one blow, crushed the flat end to a blunt button, and plunged the finished nail in a waiting bucket of water.

Then he began again.

Several hours of mindless, sweaty pounding later, he had a pile of nails large enough to rebuild the village should a mammoth wave wash it all out to sea. And he still hadn't driven the feel of her skin from his mind.

So soft. So warm. Scented with dusting powder and her natural sweetness.

Damn his eyes. Damn all his senses.

Aaron banked the fire in the forge. He put all his tools away, washed at the pump, and saddled his mare for a ride into the village. He wasn't usually a hard-drinking man, but tonight he needed a pint or three.

After tethering his horse on the village green, he made his way through the familiar red-painted door of the Bull and Blossom. He hunkered down on a stool in the nearly empty tavern, stacking his fists on the bar.

"Be right with you, Mr. Dawes," the serving girl sang out to him from the kitchen.

"Take your time," he answered.

He had all night. No one was waiting for him. No one.

He lowered his head and banged his brow against the anvil of his stacked fists. *Coarse. Mutton-brained. Lout.*

"Dawes, you need a woman."

Aaron's head whipped up. "What?"

Fosbury, the tavern keeper, plunked a tankard of ale on the counter. "I hate to say it. Unhappy bachelors are better for my profits. But you need a woman."

"Tonight, a woman is not what I need." He took a long draught of ale.

"She came around the forge today, didn't she?"

Aaron lifted the tankard for another sip. "Who did?"

"Miss Highwood."

Aaron choked on his ale.

"It's no secret." Fosbury wiped down the counter. "Ever since she showed up in this village, you've had eyes for her. Not surprising. You're a man in your prime, and she's the prettiest thing to grace Spindle Cove in some time."

Aaron scrubbed his face with both hands. Curse him, Fosbury had too many things right.

From the first sight of her, he'd been utterly smitten. He had a weakness for finely wrought things, and by God, Diana Highwood was just so . . . perfect. In any other village, men might sit on these barstools and debate which woman deserved the honor of most comely in town. In this tavern, that debate would begin and end over a single sip of ale. Diana Highwood took the honors, without question. She had the face of an angel. Delicate and beautiful.

But though her fair looks might have caught his eye, other qualities had snared his heart.

It had all started the night they'd spent struggling to save Finn Bright's life. The youth had lost his foot in an explosion, and he'd been brought to the forge for surgery. Miss Highwood wasn't a healer or a nurse, but she'd insisted on staying to help. Bringing water, mopping blood, dabbing the sweat of delirium from Finn's brow.

That was the night Aaron had learned the truth of Diana Highwood. That her delicacy was only skin deep—but the beauty went all the way through.

The longer she lived in this village, the more he found in her to admire. She wasn't only beautiful; she was brave as well. Then determined, intelligent, charitable. By now, she was some sort of paragon in his mind, and Aaron worried that long after she left, he'd be comparing every woman he ever met to her.

And they'd all fall short.

He stretched his hand, regarding it in the dim light. The pad of his thumb still burned where he'd brushed a lock of hair from her neck. It felt singed, cinder-kissed. He pressed it against the cool tankard, but it still throbbed, hot and achy.

Damn, he was hot and achy everywhere. He'd let this attraction get away from him, and now she was deep under his skin. In his blood, it seemed.

"She's not for you," Fosbury said.

"I know it. I know it well." And if he'd been harboring any other thoughts, her frantic escape today would have driven them out of his head.

"She's not the only woman in this village."

"I know that, too. It's just . . . so long as she's living here, I can't seem to take an interest in anyone else."

Fosbury leaned close over the counter and lowered his voice. "The answer could be right under your nose. You don't have to look far."

The tavern keeper tilted his head in the direction of the serving girl, who'd emerged from the kitchen with a rag to wipe the tables clean. She cast a friendly smile in Aaron's direction, and he returned the greeting with a nod.

When she was out of earshot, Aaron muttered, "You want me to court Pauline Simms?"

"She'd make you a good wife. Hardworking, clever with sums. She's grown up well, too." Fosbury rapped the countertop with his knuckles, then drifted away. "Think about it."

Under the guise of stretching his neck, Aaron had another look at the girl.

He thought about it.

Fosbury was right. Pauline Simms was the sort of woman he *ought* to set his sights on. She was one of his kind. Working class, the daughter of a farmer. As Fosbury said, she was quick with her hands and her wits. She'd be a help to any man with a trade. Admittedly, she had a few rough edges, but nothing some care and time wouldn't smooth.

As he watched, she tipped over a decorative plate, muttering, "Bollocks."

He smiled. But even though they were only four years apart in age, and even though she'd long grown into a woman—a pretty one, at that—Aaron couldn't look at Pauline Simms without seeing the gap-toothed, freckled girl who'd grown up a year behind his own sister.

That was the problem with a village this small. Every available woman felt like a sister to him. Or maybe it was his own circumstances that had permanently cast him in the big-brother role.

When his father had died ten years ago, slumped over

the anvil from a heart attack, it didn't matter that Aaron was barely seventeen. He'd needed to become the man of the family, and quick. He'd taken over the forge, working hard to support his mother and sisters.

When Spindle Cove became a retreat for well-bred young ladies, some of the other men had groused about the village being overrun . . . but it suited Aaron fine. By then, both his sisters had married, and they and his mother had moved away. So he liked having the visiting young ladies around. He mended their locks and buckles; they purchased the silver and copper trinkets he made in his spare time. It was like having a flock of little sisters to replace the ones he so sorely missed.

Except for Diana Highwood.

He'd never felt brotherly toward her.

He drained his ale. It wasn't strong enough. "Pauline?"

She looked up from mopping a table clean. "Yes, Mr. Dawes? Anythin' else you need?"

"Bring me a whiskey, will you?"

CHAPTER 2

As was their habit, all the ladies residing in the Queen's Ruby rooming house gathered in the parlor after dinner. A roaring fire kept the chill at bay.

Even now, hours after leaving the forge, Diana was still out-of-sorts. The bit of needlework she'd been working on wouldn't come out right, and she'd lost patience with it.

She'd lost patience with herself.

She'd spent the better part of two years girlishly infatuated with Aaron Dawes, all the while trusting nothing could come of it. He'd mended every scrap of metal she possessed— sometimes two or three times—showing her nothing but neighborly patience.

Until today. Today, he'd shown her something much more.

And she'd panicked and fled. Not even politely, but as if he were an ogre. She was certain he'd been wounded by her hasty retreat.

Now she'd have to avoid him for as long as she remained in the village. How unbearably awkward.

She gave up on stitching and cast a glance out the window. Through the dark and wet, she saw a familiar black mare grazing on the village green.

He must be at the tavern tonight.

"This dratted rain," her sister Charlotte moaned. "It's setting us all on edge. Two weeks now with no country walks, no gardening, no romps through the castle ruins. No amusement at all."

"I don't mind rain." This came from Miss Bertram, a young lady new in Spindle Cove this spring. "I always loved spending rainy days with Mr. Evermoore."

Charlotte stifled a giggle.

Diana gave her sister a pleading look. *Don't. Don't make fun.*

Spindle Cove was a haven for odd, unconventional, and misunderstood young ladies. But even among misfits, Miss Bertram didn't quite mix. She was hard to know—mostly because she had nothing to say that didn't involve her relationship with this mysterious rogue, Mr. Evermoore.

"My parents didn't approve of Mr. Evermoore," Miss Bertram went on. Her dark eyebrows stood out like bold punctuation on an otherwise unremarkable face. "They don't understand our attachment. That's why I'm here, you know."

Charlotte giggled again.

Miss Bertram's dark eyebrows gathered in a wounded line. "No one understands. No one." She lifted her book before her face and turned a page with a snap.

Charlotte buried her face in her hands and convulsed with silent laughter.

"Stop," Diana whispered. "You shouldn't poke fun."

"Who needs to poke it? She offers it up so readily." Charlotte mimicked in a high whisper, "Oh, Mr. Evermoore. No one understands our love."

"She's hardly the first young woman to lose her head over an unsuitable man."

"What about an imaginary one? I'd wager anything that Mr. Evermoore is Mr. Never-Was. She just wants to impress us."

"All the more reason to show her kindness."

Charlotte said lightly, "That's the lovely thing about being your sister, Diana. You're kind enough for us both."

Diana felt a twinge of guilt. She hadn't treated Mr. Dawes very kindly today. In her agitation, she jabbed at the fabric and pricked her finger. "Drat."

She scouted her immediate surroundings for her thimble. It wasn't in her sewing basket, nor caught in the folds of her skirt. "Have you seen my thimble, Charlotte?"

"No. When did you have it last?"

"This afternoon, I think. When we went to the Bull and Blossom for tea. I'm sure it was in my kit, but I can't find it now."

Before they could expand their search, the door creaked open, admitting a sharp blast of icy wind. Their visitor appeared in the entry, throwing back her hood to reveal a shock of white-blond hair.

Sally Bright shook off her damp cloak and hung it on a hook. Her cheeks were pink. "I brought over the post. It was dreadful late today on account of the muddy roads, and I couldn't wait for you ladies to come collect it tomorrow."

Diana smiled to herself. Together with her brothers, Sally

kept the All Things shop, and she was the biggest gossip in the village. If she'd taken the trouble to bring over the post, that must mean there was something of interest in it.

Something she couldn't steam open, read, and reseal with no one the wiser.

Sure enough, Sally held out a packet tied with string. "Look. It's a lovely great package from our dear Mrs. Thorne. And it's addressed to all of you."

"Something from Kate?" Charlotte leaped to take the packet and wrestle with the strings. "Oh, how wonderful."

Kate Taylor had been the village music tutor until last summer, when she'd married Corporal Thorne—now Captain Thorne—and moved away to follow his rising career. Though everyone in Spindle Cove was happy for them, Kate's lively spirit and melodies were sorely missed.

"There's a packet of handwritten booklets," Charlotte said, sorting the contents. "And a letter. I suppose I should read it first."

"Aloud, if you will," said Sally.

All the ladies gathered close.

Charlotte's eyes widened as she scanned the page. "She sends us all greetings from Ambervale."

This news was met with a general murmur of excitement.

Ambervale was the estate of the eccentric Gramercy family, headed by the Marquess of Drewe. Kate was the Gramercys' cousin by some tenuous, and rather scandalous, connection. Nevertheless, they'd welcomed her to the fold . . . and now into their house, which was situated just a few hours away.

"I hope this means she's coming to visit," Diana said.

"Even better," said Charlotte. "Lord Drewe is inviting *us* to visit *them*. All of us."

"A ball!" Mama cried. "Oh, I knew it. I knew Lord Drewe would want another chance at you, Diana."

"Mama, I'm sure this means nothing of the sort."

"Of course it does! Such a handsome, elegant man. The two of you made a striking couple. Everyone could see it."

Not again. When the Gramercys had been in Spindle Cove last summer, Mama had made the most embarrassing remarks to poor Lord Drewe, always angling for a match between him and Diana.

Charlotte gave them all a superior look. "Shall I read the letter, or would you prefer to spend the evening guessing at its contents?"

Mama closed her mouth and sat quietly.

"She writes, 'Captain Thorne and I are guests at Ambervale for the month. Thus far, it has rained every day. I can only imagine that you are enduring the same tiresome weather in Spindle Cove. My dear cousins, Lady Harriet and Lady Lark, have concocted the enclosed scheme.'"

"A *scheme?*" Mama echoed. "What sort of invitation is this?"

"'Since Lord Drewe decided dancing and cards would be poor form during Lent, the ladies devised a theatrical.'"

Miss Bertram perked with interest. "Mr. Evermoore is very fond of the theater."

Charlotte read on, summarizing for the group. "It's a command performance, and we are the players. On Thursday next, Lord Drewe will send his carriages to convey the Spindle Cove ladies to Ambervale. We must arrive prepared to present the enclosed play, which Lady Harriet believes will have unique devotional meaning for the season."

Diana reached for one of the booklets, reading the title aloud. " '*Doomed by Virtue: The life and death of St. Ursula.*' "

Mama clucked her tongue. "That Lady Harriet is very strange."

"She's brilliant," Charlotte said. "What other play is going to have a dozen female parts? All those handmaidens. And no one can complain that such an amusement is improper. Our cathedral is named for St. Ursula, after all."

"You'll need to be busy with costumes and such," Sally said, happy at the prospect of imminent sales. "I'll open the shop early tomorrow."

The mood in the room brightened as copies of the play were passed around and plans for rehearsals, costumes, and props volleyed back and forth.

Diana had to agree with her sister. Lady Harriet *was* brilliant. This was what they all needed—a source of excitement for the coming week, and an outing to look forward to. A diversion. Perhaps it would take her mind off Mr. Dawes.

"Of course, Diana must be Ursula."

Diana startled. "Why must I be Ursula?" She had been hoping for the most minor of the handmaiden roles.

Sally lifted one shoulder in an *isn't-it-obvious* shrug. "Pure. Beautiful. Saintly. That's you, Miss Highwood, isn't it?"

No, Diana wanted to object. *No, it isn't. You're looking at a woman who ogled a man's brawny forearms this afternoon. And ran from his kiss out of cowardice, not virtue.*

For the first time since the announcement of this theatrical scheme, her mother showed genuine enthusiasm. "Yes, Diana must be Ursula. With Lord Drewe playing the role of her bridegroom. It's perfect."

Diana pinched the bridge of her nose. "Mama, you do understand how this story ends? How Ursula achieved her sainthood? She is beheaded by Huns and dies a virgin."

"True." Charlotte leafed through the play. "But then, so do her handmaidens. They all die virgins."

"There, see? At least you'll be the *leading* virgin," Mama said. "And you'll have the best costume. A *bridal* costume. That will set Drewe's mind turning."

"I tell you, it won't." In an attempt to end the conversation, Diana renewed her search for her thimble. Where could it have gone?

With a smug harrumph, Mama propped her feet on a low stool and settled her petticoats. "You are meant to be a nobleman's wife, Diana. I have always known it. My intuition—"

"Forgive me, but your intuition must be flawed," Diana replied, peering under a chair. "You've been predicting my lofty match for years. During that time, no fewer than three unmarried noblemen have resided in this village. None of them expressed the slightest desire to wed me."

"Because you did not encourage them! If you fancy a gentleman, you must let him know. Not in words, of course, but in the language of female subtleties."

Female subtleties? Mama possessed all the subtleties of an elephant on parade. She brazenly thrust Diana into the path of every available gentleman.

Meanwhile, the one man Diana found attractive wasn't a

gentleman at all but the village blacksmith. And apparently subtleties weren't her strong point, because he'd seen right through her.

Aaron Dawes could tell her thoughts weren't saintly.

But he'd wanted to kiss her anyway.

She glanced out the window again. His mare was still outside the tavern.

"I'm not unfeeling, Mama. Merely careful. You know I've had to be."

She touched a hand to the chain around her neck and the small bottle of tincture hanging there. It was her talisman. The medicine inside was meant to help her in a breathing crisis. She'd suffered from asthma ever since she was a small girl.

For most young people, tantrums and tears and wild whoops of joy were all normal parts of childhood. Not so in Diana's case. Not only had she been kept inside, prevented from running and playing and stomping through the snow, but she'd also been schooled to temper her feelings. No outbursts of any kind.

Emotions were too dangerous.

Charlotte settled next to her, crushing into the same chair and fondly stroking Diana's shoulder. She murmured, "You know how I hate to agree with Mama, but I don't think she's entirely wrong. You should be Ursula. And flirt with Lord Drewe if you feel like it. This is your time to take the lead."

"My time to be a martyred medieval virgin?"

"Your time to do whatever you please. You know what Susanna said last year about your asthma. It isn't coming back. And if you don't need to worry about dying any longer . . . don't you want to start living?"

She pushed a copy of the play into Diana's hand. "Here. Take whatever role you choose. Except Cordula. I want to be Cordula. She gets the most gory execution."

Diana stared at the play for a moment. Then she handed the folio back at her sister. "Not now. I . . . I think I've remembered where I left my thimble." She rose from the chair.

"Really? Where?"

Diana went to fetch her cloak from a peg by the door. "At the Bull and Blossom. I'll just run over to get it."

"But the rain!" her mother called.

Diana closed the door on her mother's objection and dashed outside.

Charlotte was right. Now that her health had mended, Diana needn't fear her own emotions any longer.

She *did* want to start living. And she was going to start tonight.

Aaron told himself his second drink would be the last.

And then he ordered one more.

Fosbury had already sent Pauline home for the evening, and the tavern keeper yawned as he slid the refilled tumbler across the bar.

"I should go," Aaron said. "It's late."

"No, take your time with it." Fosbury knotted his apron at the waist. "I've some yeast dough to start for tomorrow's bread. Give a shout if you need anything."

He disappeared into the kitchen, whistling as he went.

Aaron had just grown accustomed to his comfortable pocket of quiet when the creak of the door ripped it open again. He turned his head, expecting to see one of the fishermen or farmers come in for a late pint.

What he saw nearly knocked him off his stool.

Diana Highwood.

She rushed through the door, slammed it closed, then stopped dead in her paces. Staring at him.

Aaron didn't know what to say, but it seemed she was waiting to hear something. He finally settled on "Good evening."

"Good evening."

Another long, uncomfortable pause.

She looked at the empty stool beside his. "Might I join you?"

Bemused, he waved a hand in invitation.

She approached the bar and settled on the seat, daintily arranging her skirts.

Aaron lifted his drink, stealing glimpses at her out of the corner of his eye. He'd spent a great many stolen moments admiring her, but tonight something was different.

She was different. He couldn't look at her tonight and see a paragon up on a pedestal. She was a disheveled girl sitting on a barstool. Damp from the rain, cheeks flushed, wisps of flaxen hair matted to her brow. She looked impulsive. Sensual.

More beautiful than ever.

Between her intoxicating looks and the fact that he was on his third whiskey, he was addled. He didn't know what she was doing here, but so long as she was sitting next to him, he was going to stare. He propped his elbow on the bar and drank in every detail of her rain-misted face, savoring.

Her gaze fell to his tumbler of whiskey. "You're having a drink?"

"Yes."

She picked up the tumbler and stared into it. "Is it brandy?"

"Actually, it's—"

Before he could get the words out, she'd lifted the glass to her lips and tossed back half the contents in one swallow.

" . . . whiskey."

She set it down. Stared at it, wide-eyed. Coughed. "Oh. So it is. Goodness."

After a moment's pause, she lifted the tumbler again.

This time, he acted. He grasped her slender wrist, cutting her draught short. "Miss Highwood, you shouldn't."

"Oh, I think I should. I think this is exactly what I need."

"But your health."

"You mean my asthma?" She set the tumbler down, and he released her wrist. "My asthma hasn't troubled me in years."

"Of course it has. That's why you're here in Spindle Cove."

She shook her head slowly. "I haven't had a breathing crisis since the one you witnessed here in this tavern. That was two summers ago. Susanna consulted with physicians in London, and she thinks I've outgrown it. People do, she said. Apparently, I'm . . . I'm cured."

She was cured? Aaron was confused. This didn't make any sense. Her breathing troubles were the reason the Highwoods had moved to this village—the sea air was beneficial to her lungs.

She fidgeted with the necklace he'd mended just that day—the one with the vial of precious tincture dangling from the chain. "I don't even need it anymore. I know in my soul, I don't. I only wear it out of habit." Her blue eyes met his. "And because you made it."

Her confession was like a punch to the jaw. It came out of nowhere and set his head spinning.

The whiskey was starting to hit her, too. He could tell from the glassy sheen in her eyes and the unsteady motions of her hands. But mostly, by the ridiculous words spouting from her lips.

He tossed a few coins on the bar and stood, putting a hand under her elbow to help her to her feet, too. "Come. I'll walk you back to the rooming house."

He didn't give her a chance to object, tucking her arm through his in a way that he hoped wouldn't look improper to anyone who might happen to see.

"You were right today," she confessed. "I'm not clumsy."

No sooner had she said it than she stumbled over the doorstep.

"Not usually." She giggled.

Giggled? He didn't remember ever hearing Diana Highwood giggle.

"I broke the necklace on purpose, just so you'd have to mend it. So I could watch you mend it." She shook her head. "That's dishonest of me, isn't it? Why would I do that? Lie to you, lie to myself."

He herded her across the lane and onto the village green. It was muddy, but the shortest route. Getting her home as quickly as possible seemed his best strategy.

"Miss Highwood, you need to rest."

"I don't need to rest. I'm cured. I'm perfectly well."

"Nevertheless, it's late. And wet. You need to be getting back to the rooming house before your mother and sister worry."

"No." She lifted a hand to her temple. "No, I don't want to go back to the rooming house. I want . . ." Her face scrunched up, and her speech gained in rapidity what it lost in coherence. "Oh, I don't know what I want. That's the problem. All my life, I've been discouraged from wanting anything. I couldn't risk Minerva's love of debate, or Charlotte's exuberance, or even Mama's nerves. I had to be calm. Delicate, cool, serene Diana. That's been me, always. No wild passions. No adventurous dreams. It seemed silly to plan for the future. For all I knew, I wouldn't live to see it."

He didn't like this talk of her dying. "But you said you're cured now."

"And then tonight . . ." Her voice broke as she gestured at the Queen's Ruby. "Tonight, my sister asked me, Don't I want to start living? And I realized I don't even know what I want from life. I know what my mother wants for me. I know what everyone else expects. But what do *I* truly desire?"

Excellent question. Aaron waited for the answer.

Her hand pressed to her chest. "Do I want to have a season in London and marry a lord? Do I want to stay here in the village and become a permanent spinster? Do I want to join a circus? I don't know, Mr. Dawes. I don't know, and it terrifies me. All those years of setting aside my emotions. My lungs are healed, but at what cost? I am a stranger to my own heart."

Raindrops spotted her face, like dew on petals. Damn, this was torture. He wanted to comfort or guard her, but he didn't know how. She wasn't his to tend.

He pulled her under the branches of a chestnut tree. The least he could do was shield her from the rain.

"There's only one thing I feel absolutely certain of," she said.

"Tell me."

Whatever it was, he vowed that she would have it.

At last she'd shaken off the manacles clapped on her—the restraints of illness and her mother's expectations. Good. Good for her. She deserved to have the things she desired.

"This afternoon." She drew close. "I wanted you to kiss me. I wanted it more than I can remember wanting anything in my life."

With that, she tilted her face to his.

And closed her eyes.

Aaron stared down at her, watching the white puffs of her breath as it left her lips. He could taste them. Little clouds of whiskey.

Her eyes fluttered open. "Didn't . . . didn't you want to kiss me, too?"

"I did."

"Then why don't you? We're alone. No one ever has to know."

He snorted at that last. "It's impossible to keep a secret in this village."

"No, it's not. I've been keeping all sorts of secrets for years. For example, sometimes I think, very hard, about how you'd look without your shirt. You never would have guessed that, would you? No one would."

He couldn't help his startled laugh.

"And I gaze at your hair." She lifted a hand, and her ungloved fingers caught a lock of his hair. "It gets long sometimes, all the way to your collar. And then one day, it will be short again. I always wonder who you've been to see."

She was half drunk, more than a little overwrought ... but her words tapped a deep well of curiosity. He'd always known there was more to her than the pretty face everyone admired. He'd known her to possess courage and a good heart. But now, he caught glimmers of other qualities. Sensuality. Jealousy. A sly sense of humor.

This was an entirely new Diana Highwood. A *real* one. And she was with him, right now, in the rain and dark.

"Won't you kiss me?" she whispered, sidling close. "Just the once?"

"The thing is, Miss Highwood, I'm not interested in kissing you just the once."

"Oh." Her face fell.

He propped one finger under her chin, tilting her face back up. "If I were to kiss you, once wouldn't be enough. I'd want to kiss you many times. In lots of places."

Her eyes flew wide. "Oh. I ... I see."

He doubted she did see. She couldn't even imagine. A few fingers of whiskey couldn't provide that much education. The carnal images in his mind could shock the silk from her stockings.

"Listen," he said, "I know you've been living in some sort of cage. And tonight, it seems you learned you've been holding the key all along. You deserve a bit of rebellion, but I can't be it. I can't be the man you wake up regretting."

"Then make the kiss good. So I won't have regrets." Smiling, she slid her arms around his neck. Her weight pitched forward.

Jesus. She could barely stay on her feet. Which, of course, meant her body was all pressed up against his. Fortunately, her woolen cloak was as thick as a horse blanket.

"Miss Highwood . . ."

"Call me Diana." She let her head fall forward, nestling into his coat.

"Diana." Until he spoke the name aloud, he hadn't known how deeply he'd wanted to call her that. *Diana, Diana.*

"You're so strong," she murmured. "And warm. You smell like soap."

"Diana, I know you. We've lived in the same small village for almost two years, and we've come through a few trials together. Let's just say I've paid attention. I won't deny I've wanted this, but not this way. You're confused, upset, and more than a little drunk. This"—he put an arm about her, steadying her—"can't happen tonight."

She clung to him, her face stubbornly buried in his coat. He embraced her, trying to keep out the chill. Not entirely selfless valiance on his part. He loved the feel of her in his arms.

He bent his head and murmured in her ear. "I'll take you home now."

She made a whimper of protest.

"No, Diana. It has to be now. Else I'll be tempted to bring you home with me instead, and then you'd be stuck. All those choices you've glimpsed tonight would disappear. Ruined, and forced to marry a craftsman? You don't want that."

She didn't answer. Just hugged him tight.

"You don't want that," he repeated more firmly.

Or *did* she?

She was silent for a few moments, which his heart stretched into hopeful lifetimes.

And then she gave her answer—a soft, unmistakable snore.

Chapter 3

The next morning, Diana woke with all sorts of regrets. They were stabbing her straight through the eyes, those regrets. Her pounding head felt like . . .

Like a blacksmith's anvil.

She groaned, putting a hand to her eyes. She had a hazy memory of coming in through the rooming house door, waving a brief good night to her mother and sister, then stumbling up to her bed. Unfortunately, her memories of throwing herself at Aaron Dawes were all too clear.

Oh, the humiliation. What he must think of her.

She pulled the coverlet up over her head, turning to bury her face in the pillow. A mistake. She couldn't hide from the memory here. As she pressed her face to the mattress, recollections of last night's embrace assailed her. His warmth, his solid strength. His honorable treatment of her when she'd cast all her good breeding in the mud at his feet.

Her head throbbed. The rest of her ached with a fierce, hopeless yearning.

"Diana?" Charlotte rapped on the door. "Are you well?"

No. No, I'm not well. I am very poorly in the head. And in the heart. Kindly go away.

"The rain's let up," Charlotte said, opening the door a crack. "Mama wants to pay a call at Summerfield. Will you join us?"

Diana was tempted to stay abed and plead headache. She wouldn't even need to exaggerate. But if there was one thing she was proud of doing last night, it was deciding that she wouldn't be defined by "delicate health" any longer.

She threw back the coverlet. "I'll join you."

She rose from bed, dressed, choked down a bit of tea and toast, and donned her sturdiest shoes. Perhaps if she walked far enough, she would leave this feeling of mortification behind.

The walk to Summerfield did loosen some of the knots in her stomach. And they all enjoyed their brief visit with Sir Lewis Finch, who told them the latest news of his granddaughter. By the time they began their walk home, the sky had lightened noticeably. Diana could almost forget the embarrassment of last night.

Almost.

"How did it go last night?" Charlotte asked.

Diana stumbled over a rock. "What do you mean?"

"Your thimble. Did you find it at the Bull and Blossom?"

The thimble. Diana shook her head. "It wasn't there."

"That's so odd."

"Not really. It's just a thimble. Thimbles go missing."

"But just this morning, Mrs. Nichols was missing her ink bottle, too. It's a mystery."

Diana smiled. Charlotte's imagination always led her to see more excitement than was truly there. "I'm sure it's a co-incidence."

"It's a tragedy," Mama exclaimed, stopping in the lane. "Oh, this cannot be borne."

"The disappearance of my thimble, a tragedy? I think I can survive it."

"No, look." Mama gestured toward the sky, where the thick blanket of clouds had parted to reveal a patch of blue—and within it, the bright, cheery face of the sun. "The sun is out. Oh, this is dreadful."

"Dreadful?" Charlotte laughed. "It's our first sunshine in a fortnight. It's marvelous."

"It is dreadful. Because your sister left the rooming house with only her cloak and no proper bonnet." She hurried to Diana's side. "Ten minutes of this, and she will freckle. Oh, and less than a week before our invitation to Ambervale. What will Lord Drewe think?"

"If he notices—which I doubt he will—he will think I've been in the sun."

"Exactly!" She tugged at the hood of Diana's cloak, drawing it up as far as it would go. "Keep your head down, Diana. Just look at your feet."

Diana lifted her head, letting her hood fall back. "But then how will I see where I'm going? I might fall on my face. I should think Lord Drewe would take more notice of bruises than he would freckles."

"Head down, I say." Mama yanked the hood up again.

"No." Diana thrust it back. "Mama, you're being ridiculous. This is a beautiful morning. I mean to enjoy it."

She braced herself for another round of Tug-o'-Hood, but Mama didn't care to play. She was distracted by the sounds of hoofbeats and carriage wheels and turned to peer down the lane.

"There is Mr. Keane with his curricle. He will save you."

"Save me? I survived years of asthma. I don't believe freckles are a terminal condition."

"Head down," she snapped. As the curricle drew near, she lifted one arm and waved to him with her handkerchief, like a drowning sailor in need of a rope. "Mr. Keane! Oh, Mr. Keane, do help!"

"Please don't trouble him."

"He is the vicar. He ought to do a good deed."

The curricle rolled to a halt in the lane. What with the strong sun and the harsh shadows, it was hard to peer into the covered bench seat—but the driver didn't seem to be the vicar. This man was rather . . . larger.

"Is there some problem?" he asked in a dark, all-too-familiar baritone.

Oh no. No. It couldn't be.

What wretched luck. Diana took her mother's advice. She drew her hood up and stared at her boots.

"Why, Mr. Dawes," her mother said, her tone wary. "What are you doing with Mr. Keane's curricle?"

"*Mama,*" Diana hissed. Good Lord, she made it sound as if he'd stolen the thing.

"And good morning to you, Mrs. Highwood," Mr. Dawes answered patiently. Out of the corner of her eye, Diana saw him tip his cap. "Miss Charlotte. Miss Highwood."

She felt his gaze on her. Now it didn't matter if she stayed out of the sun. A blush this furious would surely stain her cheeks for a month.

"Mr. Keane asked me to mend the axle," he explained. "I'm out for a short drive to test the repair before I return it. Is something wrong?"

As she listened to her mother carry on about the tragedy of sunshine and the need to keep her daughter's complexion unmarred for Lord Drewe, Diana squirmed with shame.

"Surely you can drive her back to the rooming house," Mama said. "I know it's a liberty, as you are a hired man. But I daresay I can grant permission in Mr. Keane's stead. It's what he would do, as a gentleman."

Mother!

In how many ways could she insult him? Mr. Dawes was not a "hired man." He was a skilled craftsman and artisan, and everyone in the village—Mr. Keane included—respected him.

Diana had to look up now. "Please don't let us trouble you, Mr. Dawes. I'm perfectly fine walking."

"Perfectly fine!" her mother squawked. "You'll be perfectly crisped."

She caught his gaze and tried to send an apologetic look. *Forgive her. And me.*

His expression was impossible to read. "I'd be glad to give Miss Highwood a ride into the village. I'm going there anyway."

"That is very good of you," her mother said. "When I see him, I will be sure to speak highly of your service to Mr. Keane. Perhaps there will be a shilling in it for you."

"Very kind of you, ma'am."

Mr. Dawes alighted from the curricle, adjusted the folding hood for maximum shade, then offered his hand to help Diana. Despite the awkwardness of the situation, she took a thrill from the feel of his hand dwarfing hers and the easy strength with which he boosted her onto the seat.

When he joined her, she pressed herself all the way to the opposite side.

"We'll see you back at the Queen's Ruby," Mother said. "Don't fret about me walking. I will be fine. Even at my age."

"I'm sure you will be," Diana muttered.

As Mr. Dawes flicked the reins and set the curricle in motion, Diana slunk down in her corner of the seat.

She learned something new as they rattled down the lane.

Awkwardness wasn't characterized by silence. Oh, no— awkwardness had a symphony all its own. The thump of an erratic heartbeat, contrasting with the steady squelch of hooves on packed mud. The roar of a thousand unspoken words piled up in one's throat, all clamoring to get loose. The sound of fence posts whooshing past—each one brought them closer to the village, and each one felt like a stinging lash of rebuke. Another opportunity missed.

Frantic emotion built in her chest. She couldn't stay quiet any longer.

"Mr. Dawes. Please let me apologize. For my mother just now. And for my behavior last night. And yesterday afternoon. I don't know what—"

He held up a hand, gently shushing her.

"Truly. You must think me the most presumptuous—"

"Nothing of the sort," he said, keeping his eyes on the road. "I'm just trying to listen for the axle. I think I heard it creak."

"Oh. I'm sorry." She bit her lip, hard. *Stop talking, ninny.*

"Have these for a moment." He passed her the reins, then bent and twisted away from her, looking over the curricle's side to observe the axle in motion.

Diana stared down at the leather braids in her hands. Then she looked at the trotting horses and the muddy road flying by beneath them.

"Mr. Dawes," she whispered, hoarse with fear. "Mr. Dawes, I've never—"

He held up that hand again, requesting silence. "Just a moment."

This couldn't wait a moment.

"Mr. *Dawes.*"

He straightened and turned to her. "What's the matter?"

"Kindly take the reins," she begged. "I don't know how to drive."

"You seem to be driving right now."

"But what if we have to turn? Or slow down? Or stop?" She tightened her grip. "Oh dear. Now they're going faster."

He eased closer to her on the seat. His arm pressed against hers. "You're doing fine. It's not a busy road, and the horses know their way." He put his hands over her wrists, shaking lightly. "Just lift the reins a bit and loosen your grip. These are good horses. They're trained to a soft touch."

He helped her position the reins, sliding them between her fingers.

"Like this?" she asked, sitting straight.

"That's just it. You're doing well."

His low, gentle voice entranced her and gave her confidence.

He showed her the commands for right and left; how to urge the horses faster and draw them to a halt. The lesson made for welcome distraction. At least they had something to discuss other than the mortifying events of yesterday.

"Every woman should learn to drive," he said. "I taught my own sisters when they were old enough. I never understood why the Spindle Cove ladies spend all those mornings shooting pistols and muskets, yet never have driving or riding lessons."

"I suppose the shooting lessons make us feel strong. In control of ourselves and our lives." At least, that's what the ladies' weekly target practice did for Diana.

He shrugged. "I'm not saying it's bad. But there's *feeling* powerful, and then there's actually taking the reins. They are a great many situations a woman might do well to drive away from. Very few where it's advisable to shoot her way out."

He was right, Diana thought. Loading and shooting a pistol might give a lady a rush of exhilaration, but this was true power. The freedom to choose her own direction, and harnessing the power to take her there.

"There, now you know how to drive." He moved back to his side of the seat. "Where do you want to go?"

Diana pulled on the reins, drawing the horses to a lurching halt in the middle of the empty lane. "I want to stop right here and apologize to you. I know you don't wish to speak of yesterday, but I cannot be easy until I say this. You were very kind to me, and I can't . . . I heard the way my mother spoke to you just now, and I need you to know I don't think of you that way. When I came to the tavern last night, I wasn't just seeking a moment of rebellion. I . . ."

She'd been staring at her hands all this time, but she forced herself to look up. At him.

His handsome features were a mask of confusion. Oh, she was making a hash of this.

"May I be honest with you?" she asked. "I think that's the best strategy. I'll just say everything I've been keeping to myself. And when it's out, it will surely sound ridiculous. We'll have a good laugh, and that will be the end of things. Can you bear it?"

His wide mouth crooked in a smile. "I can bear far worse."

"I . . ." *Out with it.* "I've been infatuated with you for quite some time. It's terrible."

"Terrible," he echoed.

"Not that *you're* terrible, of course. That 's not what I mean. I think you're remarkable. I'm the terrible one. It all started that night of Finn's accident. You were so confident and so strong. Just did what needed to be done, and no wavering."

"That night? Believe me, I was wavering. On the inside, I was wavering."

"I never would have known it." She laughed a little. "Of all the places to develop an infatuation. Making eyes at a man over an amputation table. It's embarrassing, isn't it?"

"Rather."

"Hardly a story a woman wants to tell her grandchildren someday."

"No, I don't suppose it would be."

She felt lighter already. "See, I told you this would all sound ridiculous. Oh, and there's so much more. You already know that I purposely broke things just to have excuses to come by the smithy. When did you start to realize the truth?"

"Just recently." His mouth tugged in a self-effacing grimace. "I'm not too sharp."

She waved off his words. "That's not true. You're so perceptive. It's evident in your finer work. I've spent hours poring over your jewelry pieces in the All Things shop. I've bought five of them."

"Five?"

"Yes. Five." She cringed. "I told Sally I was sending them to friends as gifts. A small taste of Spindle Cove, I said. But I never meant to give any of them away. I kept them all for myself. It was so stupid of me, because once I'd said they were gifts, I couldn't be seen wearing them. And if I kept them in my jewelry box, Charlotte would find them—she's always going through my things without permission. So I resorted to keeping them in the chest with my trousseau. They're wrapped up in a tablecloth."

"You have five of my pieces in your trousseau?"

"Well, only four."

"Where's the other one?" he asked.

She shook her head and pressed a hand to her cheek. "Oh, this is where it gets truly mortifying. There was one I couldn't bear to put away. But I couldn't gather the courage to wear it, either. So I took it off its chain and sewed little pockets into my frocks. Every morning, I slip it in as I'm dressing, and at night, I tuck it . . ." She buried her face in her hands.

"Where?" He sounded as if he was enjoying this now.

"Under my pillow," she moaned into her hands, knowing he'd laugh. "As if I'm a girl of fourteen."

He did laugh, but he did it good-naturedly.

"I admire all your work, but that one is my favorite. From the moment I saw it in Sally's display case, I knew I had to have it. It just . . ." She'd come this far. No turning back now. "It seemed made for me."

He was quiet for a moment. "Was it a little silver pendant with a quatrefoil design?"

She nodded. "Yes."

"Then you had it right," he said. "So long as we're being honest. It was made with you in mind."

Her heart turned over in her chest. "Oh."

"I do all my best work with you in mind. I never questioned why you came by the forge because I was just pleased you came. I didn't want you to stop. And that night with Finn? That's when it started for me, too."

They stared at each other. His dark eyes held her rapt.

"I find you terribly handsome," she blurted out. Because it was the only thing left unsaid.

He rubbed the back of his neck. "I would tell you you're the kind of lovely that's unfair to roses and sunsets. But I don't think this honest conversation is working the way you hoped."

"No. It's not. We were meant to be laughing, but none of this seems ridiculous. In fact, it feels more serious by the moment."

To know that her attraction hadn't been one-sided—that she'd been right about those long, searching looks he'd given her now and then . . . The vindication buoyed her spirits, and a delicious tingle ran from her scalp to her toes. But from there, she didn't know what happened next.

Evidently, he had some ideas.

He took the reins from her hands and secured them on the dash rail. Then he gathered her in his arms and drew her close.

Her heart stuttered. This was really going to happen.

She'd run from his kiss the first time.

The second time, she'd begged him for it.

This time, she'd learned her lesson. She did nothing but remain absolutely, perfectly still.

And it worked.

His lips touched hers, imparting that unique blend of strength and tenderness she was coming to treasure. To crave.

But all too soon, he lifted his head. "Have you been kissed before?"

"I don't know whether to say yes or no. Which answer will make you do it again?"

"Oh, I'm going to do it again." His thumb stroked her cheek. "Just wanted to know how slow to take things."

"A little faster would be fine." She'd been waiting twenty-three years, after all.

His answer was a thrilling, sensual growl. "As you like."

He renewed the kiss with a series of rough presses of his mouth to hers. Warm friction teased her lips apart, and his tongue swept between them.

The invasion was startling. She felt as though the ground had gone to liquid beneath her, and now she was adrift on unfamiliar seas. Far outside the boundaries of her experience.

As if he sensed her uncertainty, his arms flexed tight, drawing her flush with his chest. Her head naturally tilted back. She was vulnerable beneath him now, and he took control, deepening the kiss. His tongue stroked hers. The grain of his whiskers rasped at the edges of her lips. Intriguing and so essentially male. She wanted to touch him, slide her fingertips down the edge of his jaw. But she lost her courage, afraid to make a mistake and bring an end to everything.

She wanted this to last and last.

When he did pull away, he made no effort to hide that he was affected, too. It was all there, in his eyes. The deep wellspring of mutual desire and need they'd barely tapped.

"Mr. Dawes," she sighed. "What do we do?"

"First, you start calling me Aaron."

She tested it. "Aaron. What do we do?"

He put space between them. "I suppose this is where I should revise the speech I started last night. Remind you that you're a gentlewoman and I'm a craftsman, and nothing can come of this. And tell you we should just go back to trading longing glances across the green and never speak of this again. But the thing is, I don't feel like giving that speech this morning."

"Oh, good," she said, relieved. "Because I'm not at all in the mood to hear it."

"We're both sober. It's a fine, clear day. You're a grown woman, and a clever one. I believe you understand the situation. And I'm going to trust that you know your own mind."

Her heart swelled. What a lovely, lovely gift. No one else had ever done the same.

He put one hand over hers. "We have something, the two of us. I don't think we could name it quite yet, much less decide what we'd do to keep it. But if you like, we can spend more time together and puzzle it out."

"I would like that. Very much."

Goodness. It was settled, then. She had a proper suitor for the first time in her life—and he was a blacksmith. If her mother learned of this, she would be taken with fits.

She added, "But we should probably be discreet. At least for now."

Something flashed in his eyes, and she was worried she'd offended him. It wasn't that she was ashamed, of course. Just careful.

She fingered the vial of tincture hanging around her neck. Old habits were difficult to break.

He reached to untie the reins. "I'd best be getting you back to the rooming house. I did promise your mother you wouldn't freckle." He gave her a wry wink. "I hear there may be a shilling in it for me."

"Wait," she said.

Before he could set the team in motion, she rose up on the curricle seat, turned, and forced down the collapsible cover so that sunlight splashed them both.

"There." She removed her cloak and settled beside him, putting her arm through his. "Now we can go."

CHAPTER 4

"I've assigned all the parts," Charlotte said, handing copies of the play to the assembled ladies in the Queen's Ruby. "We'll read through it once this morning."

"Heaven knows, there's nothing else to do," lamented Miss Price, looking out the window at another rainy day.

Diana looked down at her copy with URSULA labeled at the top. "Really, I didn't think this was settled. Why am I playing Ursula?"

Charlotte said, "It's the easiest role in the play, I promise you. The rest of us will be running about screaming and pleading for our lives, and you just stand there and look pure."

Diana lifted a brow. Pure? Would they still find her the ideal person for this role if they knew she'd been kissing Mr. Dawes in the vicar's curricle yesterday?

No, not kissing Mr. Dawes. Kissing *Aaron*.

Aaron, Aaron, Aaron.

"*Diana.*"

She shook herself. "I'm sorry, what?"

"It's your line."

She scanned the first page and found her part, then read aloud in an even voice. "Oh, wreck and woe. My father hath betrothed me to the son of a heathen king. I should sooner die than be so defiled."

"Do speak up, Diana," her mother chided from across the room. "No one can hear you. Imagine Lord Drewe is standing just offstage, waiting for his cue."

"And put emotion into it," Charlotte added. She stood and flung one arm to the side, pressing the other wrist to her brow. "Oh, wreck and WOE. I should sooner DIE."

Diana sighed. "I don't think I possess the dramatic talent for this."

"Of course you do."

"Well, perhaps I just don't feel equal to it today."

"Are you ill?" Mama asked sharply.

Diana paused. She'd promised herself she wouldn't hide behind this excuse any longer. But she didn't want to be sitting here in the rooming house when she could be with Aaron.

Kissing Aaron. *Touching* Aaron. *Embracing* Aaron and feeling surrounded by his big, strong arms.

She had no heart to play the martyred virgin right now.

"I knew it," Mama wailed. "Oh, I knew that sun would do you an ill turn. No more rehearsal for you today. Go straight upstairs and rest. I will not have you falling ill when it's time for our outing to Ambervale. Do you have any more of that infusion from Lady Rycliff?"

"I'm sure I don't need an infusion, Mama. But perhaps I will go." She turned to Miss Bertram. "Would you be so kind as to read my part for today?"

Miss Bertram's eyebrows rose in alarm. "Oh, I . . . I don't know."

"I think you would make a marvelous Ursula. And you would be doing me a great favor."

The girl took the booklet from Diana's hand, smiling shyly. "Well, Mr. Evermoore does love my reading voice."

"I'm sure he does."

Diana tried to soothe her conscience as she left the room. She hadn't lied. Mama had merely assumed, wrongly, that she felt ill. Just like she assumed, wrongly, that Diana would follow her instructions to go upstairs and rest.

But she didn't.

Instead, she gathered her cloak and slipped out the rear door.

As she neared the smithy, a giddy flutter rose in her chest. No horses or wagons in the front meant she'd likely caught him alone. A sheen of perspiration rose on her brow even before she entered the steamy, spark-filled forge.

She entered to find Aaron not pounding at the anvil but hunched over a bit of fine metalwork at his worktable.

"Good morning," she said, swaying her skirts a bit.

He looked up only briefly and gave her a curt "Good morning" before returning his concentration to his task. "Sorry you've caught me in a busy moment. I can't leave this, or it will cool unfinished."

"Of course. Should I come back another time?"

A furrow formed in his heavy brow. "No, don't go. Unless you want to."

"I'd like to stay." She settled on her usual stool. "If I won't be troubling you."

Now he looked up, and his dark eyes caught hers. "You could never be any kind of trouble."

Never mind the roaring forge, that look sent heat rushing through her. Oh, dear. And here she was, caught without her fan.

He returned to his labor, and she sat quiet and still. She did love watching him at his work. This was different from his display of brawn and sweat she'd admired the other day. When he worked with fine metal, all that power was pushed through a narrow funnel of concentration.

The result was passion. He had an artist's passion for his creations. She touched the quatrefoil pendant in her pocket.

"There."

He set the piece aside and wiped his brow with his shirtsleeve. He left a black smudge of soot on his temple, and she found it strangely enticing. A mark of that passion, emblazoned on his skin. It spoke of virility in a primal way.

"What are you making?" she asked.

He showed her a silver bracelet, formed of two twining vines. "It's a special order for a jeweler in Hastings."

"You've been selling your work in Hastings?"

He nodded. "Rye and Eastbourne, too. I'm hoping to expand to Brighton soon."

"And London after that?"

He shrugged. "Perhaps. But there's only one of me. There's a limit to how much I can do on my own."

"Have you thought about taking on an apprentice?"

"It's not working the forge that I need help with, so much

as everything else. Fosbury says what I really need is a wi—"

He cut off the word, but Diana completed it in her mind.

What I really need is a wife.

It made sense. Marriage was a partnership in any social class. Among gentry, the lady's contribution was a dowry or well-placed connections. As a craftsman, Aaron would do well to marry a woman with practical skills to help him manage his household and his business.

Skills women like Diana didn't possess.

They traded awkward glances, and they both seemed to be thinking the same thing. What were they doing here? He wasn't the kind of suitor her mother would accept, and she couldn't be the wife he needed. If marriage was impossible, they were only flirting with heartbreak and scandal.

Still, she couldn't bring herself to leave.

We have something, he'd said yesterday, and he was right. Diana wasn't ready to give up on it yet.

He went back to his work, raking the fire and pumping the bellows that fueled the forge. "Much as I'd like to take the day off and spend it with you, I have to finish this piece. I've promised to deliver it tomorrow."

"I understand. Is there any way I can help?"

"That's kind of you to offer, but I'm not going to have you hauling wood and water."

"Why not? I helped with such things the night Finn was hurt."

"Aye, but that was an emergency. If I hadn't been so preoccupied, I never would have allowed it."

"If you'd tried to send me away, I wouldn't have listened."

She had a tenacious streak. There had to be *something* she could do. "Have you eaten your noon meal?"

He shook his head.

"Then that's what I'll do. While you finish that piece, I'll prepare a meal. Then we'll sit down to eat and have time to talk, but I won't feel I've distracted you from your work."

He looked uncertain.

"Aaron, please. Let me do this. You did say you'd trust that I know my own mind."

"So I did." He blew out his breath and wiped his hands on a rag. "Very well, then."

He turned to the hearth and scooped some red-hot embers with a tiny shovel, then handed the shovel out to her.

She moved to take it, though she wasn't sure what she was supposed to do with it next.

"For the fire," he explained.

"Yes, of course." Of course. How could anyone cook without a fire?

"One of the fishermen brought me something fresh from the catch this morning, and there's fresh butter and cream, as well. Potatoes and onions in the bin. Poke about the cabinets, and I'm sure you'll find whatever else you need."

"I could do with a kiss. Will I find one of those in the cabinets?"

"That I have right here." He tilted his head and gave her a brief, yet exhilarating, kiss.

She clutched the scoop of glowing coals. "I'll be just fine, you'll see. Now back to work with you."

She turned and headed toward the rear door of the forge.

Beyond it, a narrow yard separated the smithy from his cottage.

"Diana?"

At the sound of her Christian name spoken in that intimate, low baritone, a thrill went through her. She nearly spilled the coals. "Yes?"

"If you need anything, you will ask?"

"Oh, of course I will," she assured him. "Don't look so worried. It's not as though I've never done this before."

Diana had never done this before.

Any of it.

Not light a fire, not clean a fish . . . and most certainly not cook a meal. But she was going to do all this today, and she was going to do it well.

She entered the cottage kitchen. It was a sparely furnished room, but orderly and clean. There was no denying it could do with a woman's touch—the curtains hanging in the window were recently laundered, but faded.

In a covered basin on the table lay, she assumed, the fish. Most likely sole or plaice, she imagined. A flat, muddy footprint of a fish that Diana would somehow need to behead. And gut. And scale and fillet and . . .

She swallowed hard.

That part could wait. She'd pare the vegetables first.

The fire, she suddenly realized. Goodness. She couldn't cook anything without a fire.

By habit, she'd never strayed too near a fireplace or stove— not only because her mother had insisted gentlewomen didn't dirty their hands with such tasks but also because Diana had feared that inhaling smoke or ash could trigger a breathing crisis.

Those worries were in the past now. She faced a different challenge today.

She cautiously carried the scoop of glowing coals to the kitchen hearth. A nearby box held some straws and dried moss. Crouching on the hearthstones, she heaped the tinder in the grate, then lifted the scoop and gently sifted a few embers atop it.

A fizzling curl of smoke rose up.

And promptly died, taking all her excitement with it.

What was she doing wrong? She thought of Aaron stoking the fire in the smithy, raking and turning the coals . . . pumping the bellows.

The bellows. That was it. A fire needed air.

She scattered another few embers over the tinder, then lowered herself almost to her belly, pursed her lips, and blew. A flurry of sparks resulted. Encouraged, she inhaled slowly, then exhaled again, careful not to overtax her lungs. This time, the little sparks swelled and caught the tinder, resulting in a few lapping tongues of flame.

Diana rose to her knees and cheered—quietly—while brushing the dust from her hands and skirts. A small triumph, perhaps, but a promising start.

Her sense of triumph quickly dampened, however, when the tinder began to flame out and she realized she had no split logs to keep the fire going. She looked around. Nothing, to either side of the hearth. Then she recalled the well-stocked woodpile outside the smithy, under the overhang.

After another slow, loving exhalation to nourish her small flames, she rose and dashed outside, gathering an armful of splits from the pile before hurrying back, all the while praying the fire wouldn't die in her absence.

She knelt before the hearth—no more care for her skirts this time—and placed the thinnest of the logs atop the burning tinder.

The flames were immediately smothered, dying in a thin plume of white, elegiac smoke.

"No," she cried. "No, no, no."

She flattened herself to the hearthstones and huffed desperately, trying to rekindle the flame.

She couldn't go back to Aaron and ask for more coals. He would know she'd failed before she'd even begun, and that she couldn't perform the most basic of household tasks. What use could she ever be to him? It wasn't as though they'd talked about marriage, but she wasn't ready to foreclose the possibility.

"Please," she begged. "Please, please. Don't go out."

And as if some pagan god of fire heard her petition, a small flame caught a notch on the underside of the wood. The fire began to gnaw at it, dripping morsels of ash.

Hosanna.

She fed the fire carefully, not daring to stray a pace from the hearth until she had a tall, respectable blaze.

When she felt it safe to rise, she gave the basin on the table a wary glance. She wasn't ready for that fish just yet.

Instead, she found a knife and set about paring vegetables and adding them to a kettle of salted water. She managed three potatoes, two carrots, and an onion with only one slice to her finger. She bound her wound with a strip of linen torn from her handkerchief. The onion made a useful scapegoat for her silly tears.

After hanging the kettle on a hook and swiveling it over the fire to boil, she could no longer postpone the inevitable.

Time to gut the fish.

She went to the table and lifted the cover from the basin.

"Ah!" With a muted shriek, she dropped the cover. It felt back with a bang.

Oh Lord, oh Lord.

Several moments passed before she could bear to lift the cover again and peer inside. She hoped to see something different this time. But no.

There it was.

It wasn't a fish.

It was an eel.

And it was still *alive*. Just angrily alive and now agitated, weaving slick, dark-green figure eights in its basin of murky water.

With a shudder, Diana covered it again. Then she drew out a chair and decided to sit and think for a while, about just how much she truly wanted this.

She closed her eyes and thought of Aaron's kiss. The strength of his arms around her. The heat of his body, and the tender mastery of his tongue coaxing hers. She remembered their driving lesson. The joy of racing down a country lane, as fast as the spring mud would allow, with the top of the curricle down.

Then she pictured that eel, filling the basin with its writhing, slippery will to live.

She just couldn't. Could she?

Diana opened her eyes and steeled her resolve. Some days, she decided, freedom meant the wind in your hair and the sun on your face and lips swollen with forbidden kisses.

And other days, freedom meant killing an eel.

She found the largest cleaver in the kitchen and gripped it in her right hand. With the left, she lifted the cover from the basin.

"I have nothing against you," she told the eel. "I'm sure you're a perfectly fine creature. But Aaron and I have something. And I'm not going to let anything stand . . . or slither . . . in the way of it."

And just as she reached in to grab the thing . . .

It *jumped*.

It jumped clear out of the basin and—to Diana's gasping horror—landed directly on her chest.

Chapter 5

Once Diana disappeared into the cottage, Aaron quickly lost himself in his work. He needed to get this piece right. If the jeweler was satisfied, it would mean a tidy sum in Aaron's pocket—and more commissions in the future.

He did this finer work because he enjoyed it; the profit had always been secondary. He lived simply, and village smithing gave him more than sufficient income to meet his needs. But he was thinking about the future now.

Thinking hard.

He didn't even realize how much time had passed until he looked up from the finished bracelet and saw it was midafternoon. Damn it. He'd left her waiting for hours.

He banked the fire, removed his apron, put away his tools, and locked the finished bracelet in his strongbox. Then he took a few minutes to wash at the pump before going inside. Wouldn't do to go in all sweaty and covered in soot.

As he worked a soapy lather over his hands and forearms, his anticipation grew. This was like a dream come true. A day's honest work at the forge, a well-made result, and Diana

Highwood waiting for him at home, ready with a warm smile and a hot meal.

He ran his hands through his dampened hair to tame it, then entered the cottage through the kitchen door.

He found the place in shambles.

The room was cold. Every dish, pot, and spoon he owned had been turned out of the cupboards, it seemed. Peelings littered the floor. The acrid stench of burned potatoes hung in the air.

And Diana sat at his table, sobbing noisily, her head buried in her stacked arms.

"My God, what's happened?" He crossed to her at once and knelt at her side. "What is it? Tell me."

"It's ruined," she cried.

"What's ruined?"

"Everything. Your meal. My life. Our chances." She hiccupped. "The eel."

"The eel?" He made attempts to soothe her, stroking her hair and back. "What happened to the eel?"

"It . . ." She squeaked out a little sob. "It got away." A fresh burst of tears muffled the remainder of her reply.

"It got away?" He struggled manfully to contain his laughter.

"I had the knife . . . and it . . . it *jumped*. I didn't know they could jump. Do you know they can jump?" She gestured wildly about her neck and head. "On my chest . . . in my hair . . . I couldn't . . ." She coughed out an indelicate sob. "I flung it off me. It landed out the window, and then it got away."

He glanced out the window she'd indicated. The weather had left the ground sufficiently wet and muddy that he could imagine an eel finding its way into a wheel rut and traveling a fair distance. It wouldn't likely get far, but it could get away.

He laughed again. "I'd say that eel earned its pardon, then."

"And then the vegetables boiled over, and the overflowed water put out the fire, and I . . . when I went to stoke it, a cinder caught me on the cheek. I'm sure it left a mark." She lowered her head to her arms again. "Everything's ruined. The meal is ruined, I am ruined. I'm too useless to be a working man's wife, and"—her shoulders quaked with another sob—"and now I'm disfigured, so no gentleman will want me. I'm going to die an old maid."

As she spoke, her voice tweaked higher and higher. Until her last word was no more than a plaintive squeak.

"An old maid?" he echoed. "Because of one meal that went awry? Diana, I don't know what to say. Other than to offer my congratulations."

"Congratulations?"

He patted her shoulder, chuckling. "I grew up with a mother and two sisters, and all of them like to talk. And that is, undoubtedly, the most feminine progression of thought I've ever heard voiced aloud. One escaped eel, make *you* a spinster?"

She sniffled.

He pulled up a chair next to hers and reached to touch her cheek. "Let me see the burn."

With reluctance, she offered her face for his view. "Is it very hideous?"

What a question. As if she could—*ever*—be anything less than beautiful in his eyes.

"This?" He pressed his thumb to the tiny red scorch mark on the gentle sweep of her cheekbone. "This is nothing. Barely noticeable, and it will fade in no time. I've had countless such burns myself."

"And you're still exceedingly handsome. So that's some comfort." She wiped her eyes with a shredded handkerchief. "You must think me ridiculous. I *am* ridiculous."

"No, you're not ridiculous. I understand."

"How? Do you worry about being an old maid, too?"

He smiled. "I know we come from different backgrounds. But we've more in common than you'd think. I was the oldest child, too. And when my father died, I had a mother and two younger sisters to look after."

"How old were you when he passed away?" she asked.

"Seventeen."

"I'm sorry. That's very young to be the man of the family."

"I was old enough to take his place at the forge, thankfully. I threw myself into the trade, because I knew it was how I could keep my family safe. Spent so much time at that anvil, when I went to bed I pounded iron in my sleep. Then one day, I was shoeing a horse and put my hand in the wrong place at the wrong time. The horse caught my thumb and bit it, hard." He lifted his hand to demonstrate. "My thumb was all black and swollen. I spent a week not knowing if the bone was crushed, too. Next to losing my father, it was the worst time of my life. I thought I wouldn't be able to work. The family would starve . . ."

"Everything would be ruined."

"Exactly."

She nodded. "I see what you're saying. You're right, we are

much the same. It's not my vanity that's pained, it's just . . . I was always raised to believe the family depended on me. That my prospects—and to put it bluntly, my face—were our security."

"So when your mind leaps from a scorched cheek to permanent spinsterhood, it's understandable. But that doesn't make it reasonable. You must realize you're not responsible for your family anymore. Not since your sister married Lord Payne."

"I know." She dried her eyes and drew in a breath. "I don't know why I'm sitting here weeping. I just wanted so badly for this meal to come out right."

Aaron put a roughened hand over her delicate one, touched by the implication of her words. She wanted more than just the meal to come out right. She wanted this to work between them, and so did he. But it wouldn't be easy.

"There's hope yet." With a fond squeeze to her hand, he stood. "Let's clean this up and make something to eat."

They worked together. While Aaron rebuilt the fire, Diana wiped the table and swept the floor—and then she ducked outside for a moment to wash her face and tame her frazzled hair. She did have *some* vanity.

She returned to find Aaron taking eggs and hard cheese from the larder.

"I hope omelette will do," he said. "I don't know any fancy cuisine, but I've become quite accomplished in bachelor cooking. Once my mother and sisters moved away, it was that or starve."

"Omelette sounds wonderful." She marveled at the way he

could carry four eggs in one hand, holding them each separate with his big fingers. "Where did they move to? Your mother and sisters, I mean."

"They both married sailors. One married a navy man, and she moved to Portsmouth. Mum went with her to help while he's at sea. The other lives over near Hastings. Her husband's a merchant sailor."

"Do you have nieces and nephews?"

"Five so far," he said proudly. He broke the last egg and added it to the bowl. "If you want to help, you could pare some shavings of that cheese."

She gathered a board and a small knife, then set about slicing the cheese as thinly as she could. Simple as the task was, she still had a near miss with the blade. His forearms were every bit as distracting in the kitchen as they were in the forge. She was entranced, watching him whisk the eggs with a long-handled fork.

He was so good with his hands in every situation. It was hard not to imagine the wonders those hands could work on *her*.

She ducked her head and finished paring the cheese.

He took a skillet from a hook and cut a lump of butter into it before carrying it over to the fire.

While he cooked the omelette, Diana sliced a loaf of bread and set the table for two. A burst of whimsy led her to gather two china candlesticks from a high shelf, dust them, and fit them with tapers.

He smiled when he saw them. "That's nice. Those don't get used often."

As they sat down to eat, she felt like she'd finally done something right.

"I've been wondering." He jabbed at his food, gathering a man-sized forkful of eggs. "So you're named Diana, for the Roman goddess of hunting."

"And virginity." Her lips quirked.

"Right." He wolfed down another bite of eggs. "And then your next sister is Minerva."

"Roman goddess of knowledge."

"So where does 'Charlotte' come in? Shouldn't she be a goddess, too?"

"She was meant to be. Those classical names were all the fashion in my mother's day, and you know my mother is always concerned with the latest fashion." She pushed the eggs around her plate. "She had the idea to name all her daughters after deities. I think Charlotte was supposed to be Venus. No, no. Vesta."

He choked on his food. "Either is cruel."

"I know, I know. My father's name was Charles, and they'd been waiting to name a son for him. But he fell ill while my mother was pregnant the third time. I think my mother knew there wouldn't be a fourth child, or any son at all. So that's how Charlotte was named Charlotte and spared the cruelty of Vesta."

He put down his fork. "I'm sure she'd rather have the cruel name if it meant having her father. I shouldn't have joked."

"Don't be sorry. Nearly everything my mother does is ripe for ridicule. But occasionally she does mean well."

They finished their simple meal all too quickly.

"Look at that," he said. "The sun's come out. Just in time to disappear again."

"I really ought to be going back to the Queen's Ruby. If I'm not there when dinner's called, they'll be worried."

He walked her outside and they stood there, side by side, watching the sun sink toward the horizon. A fiery red ball, painting the clouds with vibrant shades of pink and orange.

"It's beautiful," she said.

"My father used to say, Christ might be a carpenter, but the Heavenly Father is a blacksmith. He melts the sun down every night and forges it again the next morning."

Diana smiled. "What a lovely thought."

"No, it's rubbish. At least that's what I decided after he died. If a good man slumps over his anvil at the age of two-and-forty, his Creator is no kind of craftsman. I inherited his forge, not his faith." His chest rose and fell in a thoughtful sigh. "But then, every once in a while, I see something so finely made, so exquisitely wrought"—he turned to her—"I can't help but wonder. Maybe he was right."

He brushed a light touch down her cheek. "Only a divine hand could make something this lovely. Christ, you're perfect."

She laughed a little. Partly because she was amused by his blend of reverent wonder and shameless blasphemy. And partly because it made her uncomfortable.

"I'm not perfect," she said. "Not inside, not out."

"You're a terrible cook. That I'll grant you. You can't hold your liquor, either. And you have questionable taste in men. So no, you're not perfect." His voice sank to a husky whisper, and his gaze dropped to her mouth. "But you're close. Close enough to restore a man's faith in miracles."

Her heart fluttered as he leaned in for a kiss.

"Dawes!" The call came from around the other side of the smithy. "Dawes, are you here?"

Diana jumped back, worried they'd been seen. And then she worried she'd offended Aaron with her swift recoil. Again.

"It's fine," he murmured.

She didn't know which of her concerns he meant to allay.

For his part, he didn't show any unease. He walked out around the smithy and greeted the man. Evidently a horse needed shoeing.

She heard Aaron speak to him. "Walk him around, and I'll be right along. Just have to fetch something from the house for Miss Highwood."

Diana patted her hands down her front. Gloves, cloak, reticule. She had everything she'd come with, but she followed him anyway.

"What was it you needed to give me?"

"This."

He lashed an arm about her waist, pressing her up against the wall and claiming her mouth in a passionate kiss. No time for preliminaries today. He took what he wanted, thrusting his tongue deep and putting his hands in places that were just this side of scandalous. The light boning of her corset pressed into her torso—the one thing holding her together, while the rest of her seemed to dissolve.

"Right," she breathed a few moments later. "I'm glad you didn't let me leave without that."

He trailed kisses toward her ear. His whiskered jaw scraped deliciously against her cheek. "I'm taking my work to Hastings tomorrow," he murmured. "Invent some reason you need to go along. Shopping. Someone to visit. Anything."

"I . . . I could do that. So long as Charlotte comes with us."

"Good." After one last kiss to her lips, he pulled away. "I'll come for you at the rooming house, first light."

He left her there, slumped breathless against the wall. Her head whirled, and God only knew where her knees had disappeared to.

She smiled weakly to herself. "I'll be waiting."

CHAPTER 6

"Why, Mr. Dawes," Charlotte said. "I almost didn't recognize you, you look so smart this morning."

Aaron pulled a face of male modesty.

"Doesn't he look smart, Diana?"

Diana smiled. "Mr. Dawes looks quite fine."

"I'm on business today," he said, tugging down the brim of his hat. "Best to look the part."

He did look splendid, Diana had to agree. He was dressed in a rich brown topcoat that made her think of melted chocolate. His freshly starched neckcloth made a delicious contrast with his bronzed skin and dark hair.

That hair was still a touch too long, curling in dark waves at his collar. Staring at it made her wistful.

They didn't have Mr. Keane's curricle today—just Aaron's own wagon. The seat was wide enough to fit three, and Diana took the middle. The morning was brisk, and he tucked a rug over their laps.

Hastings was almost two hours' distance away, and they passed the first hour or so in near silence. Which was not to say that no communication was happening. One side of Diana's body—the side pressed against him—had developed a manner of speaking all its own. They were having a whole conversation in subtle exchanges of heat and pressure and "accidental" brushes of arm against arm, knee against knee. Each touch electrified her. She had to ration her glances in his direction so as not to give Charlotte any idea.

The secret pleasure of their flirtation made her giddy. They weren't even halfway to their destination, and already this was her favorite outing in years.

"Lud, you two are silent," Charlotte finally declared. "We must talk about *something*."

"I'm glad we've had this break in the rain," Diana said.

"And not the weather!" Charlotte complained. "I'm exhausted of everyone discussing the weather."

"What is it you'll be needing in town?" Aaron asked. "Where can I drop you when we reach Hastings?"

"We must visit the draper's first," Charlotte answered. "That's our main errand. We need yards and yards of white for Diana's costume, and there wasn't enough in the All Things shop."

"Miss Highwood's wearing a costume?"

Diana forgot she hadn't told him about the theatrical. Whenever they'd been alone together, there had been too many other things to discuss. And too many kisses to share.

"Yes, that's why we're going to Ambervale on Thursday," Charlotte explained. "We're presenting a theatrical. A pantomime on the life and death of Saint Ursula. I'm playing Cordula, and Diana is playing the lead."

"Oh, is she?" Aaron slid her an amused look. "Now that would be something to see."

"You should come," Charlotte said eagerly. "Everyone's coming. Captain Thorne will be there, of course. And I just received a letter from Minerva yesterday. She and Lord Payne will be coming down from London to attend."

"I might like to see them. What do you think, Miss Highwood?" he asked. "Would I be welcome?"

"I suppose. So long as you promise not to laugh."

When they reached Hastings, Aaron saw them to the draper's before taking his wagon to the mews and completing his business. Diana and Charlotte spent the next hour debating sateen versus crepe, then purchasing great spools of ribbon and gold braid to make headdresses for each of Ursula's eleven handmaidens.

"When he's playing Prince Meriadoc, do you think Lord Drewe will wear a codpiece?" Charlotte whispered.

"What a question! I'm sure I don't want to notice it if he does."

"Well, he's going to notice you." Charlotte draped a length of white brocade over Diana's shoulder. "You'll be stunning."

Uncomfortable with that line of conversation, Diana took the fabric and folded it away. She moved on to the display cases. "I must find a new lorgnette for Mama. Hers has disappeared."

Her sister clucked her tongue. "I tell you, something strange is going on at the rooming house. I think we have a thief in the Queen's Ruby."

"I think you just enjoy believing so."

"I have my eye on Miss Bertram. She's such an odd duck."

"Well. Mr. Evermoore must like odd ducks."

Charlotte just laughed. "Speaking of birds, I'm going to have a look at the plumes."

Her sister drifted away, and Diana concentrated on the display of lorgnettes. They didn't have any that matched the style of Mama's missing one, so she was left to choose the next best. She was just about to ask the shopgirl to bring out two for comparison when a man clad in dark chocolate brown approached her and interrupted in a deep voice.

"I beg your pardon, miss."

Her heart skipped a beat.

Aaron.

She turned to him, taking his cue and playing as though they were strangers. "Yes, sir?"

"Might I ask your opinion, as a lady?"

She looked him down, then up. "I should be glad to help if I can be of service."

He drew to the side, motioning for her to follow. He paused over a case filled with beaded reticules and lace gloves and tooled ivory fans.

"I'd like to buy a gift for my sweetheart," he said. "And I'm not sure what she'd like. I thought perhaps you might be so good as to help me choose."

A helpless smile tugged at her lips. He didn't need to buy her anything, but she couldn't deny the thought made her dizzy with joy.

Until Charlotte popped between them. "Mr. Dawes, you have a sweetheart? Who is it? Who?"

Aaron watched as Diana's cheeks paled. She gave him a look of pure panic.

"Do tell, do tell." Miss Charlotte bounced on her toes. "Who is your sweetheart, Mr. Dawes?"

"I . . ."

He didn't know what to say. He didn't want to lie, but clearly Diana hadn't told her sister anything about the two of them. That struck him as a mite strange—his own sisters had told one another everything about their romances. But they were closer in age than the eldest and youngest Highwoods were. And more to the point, they'd never gone courting with young men from a different social class.

"Charlotte, don't harass him so," Diana chided. "Is your business complete, Mr. Dawes?" She was clearly anxious to change the subject.

"Yes, thank you. And your shopping?"

"Nearly done." She called to the shopgirl and asked her to wrap up one of the lorgnettes.

"We have some time before we need to start back," Aaron said. "I thought perhaps the three of us could take some luncheon at—"

"But you haven't purchased your sweetheart's gift yet," Charlotte said.

God, the girl was like a bulldog with a bone.

"Do tell us who it is, and we'll help you choose. Is it Sally? Pauline? Oh! I know. Gertrude, the upstairs maid from Summerfield."

Aaron shook his head. "None of those."

Charlotte snapped her fingers. "One of the Willett girls.

Or that miller's daughter from the next parish. What's her name again? Betsy?"

He shook his head.

"Do we know her?" she asked.

"I . . . I'm fairly certain you do."

Diana gathered her purchase from the shopgirl and thumped her sister with it. "Charlotte, stop. You're embarrassing him."

Embarrassing her, too, Aaron would warrant.

"We'd be glad to take some luncheon," she went on. "Thank you very much for the suggestion, Mr. Dawes."

He was quiet over their meal of pigeon pie. He didn't know what to make of her reluctance to tell the truth. She wasn't ready to tell anyone, obviously. He supposed it was understandable, this soon. But would she *ever* be ready? That was the larger question.

Perhaps she didn't see matters going that far.

Aaron surreptitiously touched the packet buried deep in his breast pocket—the small quantity of gold and gemstones he'd accepted in payment from the jeweler. He'd requested compensation in materials rather than coin, thinking he'd make something special with it.

Like maybe a ring.

But now he was feeling like a fool. If Diana didn't even feel ready to tell her own sister about them, Aaron was getting too far ahead of himself.

He lifted his ale and regarded her over it. Like she did so often, she fidgeted with the slender chain always about her neck and the vial of tincture at the end of it.

Except . . .

He blinked and looked closer.

She wasn't wearing the vial on her chain today. Instead, he saw his pendant. The quatrefoil one he'd made for her. The one she'd been hiding in pockets and under pillows for months. Until today.

It wasn't a public confession. But it was something, that.

He drained his ale and thumped the tankard on the table. "If you don't mind," he announced, "I've an errand on our way back to Spindle Cove. Someone I promised I'd call on today."

Charlotte perked with interest. "Is it your sweetheart?" And close on the heels of her question, "Ow!"

He was certain Diana had kicked her under the table.

"No, Miss Charlotte, it's not my sweetheart. It's my sister."

CHAPTER 7

"Aaron Jacob Dawes, what are you doing?" Jemma chased him around the kitchen, flogging him with a damp rag and scolding him in shouted whispers. "I could have your hide, bringing such ladies around to my house with no notice."

He held up his hands in innocence. "Don't be angry. They're fine."

His sister peered through the doorway into the small sitting room, where Diana and Charlotte were sitting with Jemma's three small children and a tray of tea biscuits.

"You're lucky I baked this morning. That's all I can say." Jemma gave him the sharp side-eye that all the Dawes women used.

"You know why I'm here." He plucked a set of shears from a drawer and handed it to her. "Let's go outside and have this done."

Aaron removed his coat and cravat, then assumed his usual seat on a stump in the back garden. The air smelled damp and green. A few early daffodils were poking through the ground.

Jemma set about clipping his hair. Several moments

passed in quiet, save for the snipping of scissors. Jemma was a stubborn woman—always had been—but insatiably curious as well. He sensed a battle going on between her desire to know and her unwillingness to ask. But if he kept silent long enough, he knew which side would win.

"So," she said finally.

He smiled at the clump of toadstools near his boot. "So."

"What exactly are you doing with this Miss High-and-Mighty-Wood?"

"She's not high and mighty."

"No, no. She's quite nice, I'm sure. And beautiful as anything. I just don't know what she's doing with you."

"She's catching a ride to and from Hastings. That's what she's doing."

"Aaron. You cannot expect me to believe that. You brought her *here*. I'm cutting your *hair*."

The violence of her snipping began to alarm him. He was afraid he'd lose the top of an ear.

He said, "Stop clucking over me like a mother hen. I'm a grown man. I'm entitled to my privacy."

She snorted. "After all the headaches you gave my Dennis, I think I've earned my turn." Her voice softened as she set the scissors aside and ran her fingers through his trimmed hair. "I just don't want to see you hurt."

He stood, turned, and looked down at her from his full height, as if to say, *You're worried about* this *getting hurt?*

She brushed the clipped hair from his shoulder. "Yes, you're big. Yes, you're strong. Big and strong don't add up to invincible. I remember too well what happened with that schoolteacher."

He sighed with annoyance. "That was ages in the past. And Miss Highwood isn't anything like that."

Years ago, Aaron had taken a liking to a schoolteacher from a nearby village. They'd done some courting; he'd made some plans. Only to learn that she'd never been interested in a future with him. She'd just been hoping to make a certain bank clerk jealous—and she'd dropped Aaron like a hot brick the moment her ploy had worked. She was married to that clerk now. They lived in Lewes, in a house with glazed windows.

"I've known Miss Highwood for nearly two years, Jemma. She's a fine person."

"Mm-hm. Fine indeed. Too fine for you. That's a lady what could marry into a fortune. A grand house. Fine carriage. Dozens of servants."

"You're not helping," he grumbled.

"Yes, I am. The best way I know how." Her brown eyes held his. "Let this one go, Aaron."

He thought of that pendant hanging about Diana's neck. The tears she'd shed at his kitchen table because she'd let his dinner escape. The sweetness of her kiss.

"I can't let her go. We have something."

Jemma huffed out her breath. "Well, whatever your 'something' is . . . I hope you're prepared to fight for it."

I am, he thought to himself.

She crossed her arms and peeked into the house again. "I'll say this for her. She's been in there counting jacks with Billy for near a quarter hour. No one would put up with that child's games unless she were related to him, or hoping to be."

Her grudging approval made him smile. It was what he'd come for, after all.

"Billy's a good boy. He has a good mum." He gave his sister a fond rub on the top of the head, just as he'd done when she was a girl. "I'll stock up your woodpile before I go."

An hour later, Diana thanked her kind—but notably wary—hostess for the tea and biscuits and expressed a wish to have a wander in the garden.

She rounded the side of the house, only to narrowly miss a collision—

With Aaron.

He had shorter hair. And three children clinging to him—a giggling niece attached to either leg, and Billy hanging from his neck. She'd obviously caught them in the middle of a favorite game.

Aaron froze, a helpless expression on his face.

"You . . ." Diana cleared her throat and said in a low, solemn voice, "Mr. Dawes, you have a little something." She motioned discreetly toward her body, indicating the position of Billy's stranglehold on his neck. "Just here."

"Oh. Do I really?"

She nodded.

"Hm." He shook his whole body, as if he were a dog just come out of a lake. All three children clung tight and laughed.

"Did that take care of it?" he asked.

"I'm afraid not."

He shook again, and the children laughed harder.

"How about now?"

"*Still* there."

"Well, then." He frowned in exaggerated concentration. "Perhaps I need a good dousing in the stream."

At that, the children squealed, released him, and ran away shrieking. Diana laughed, too.

He stood tall and straightened his clothing. "Sorry to have taken so long."

"Not at all. Please don't apologize."

"Jemma's husband is at sea for months at a time. I try to come by every so often to keep the woodpile stocked, fix the leaks and sticking doors . . ."

"Chase the children around the garden," she finished for him.

His wide mouth tipped in a lazy, devastating smile. "That, too."

Diana could have sworn she felt her womb shiver. What an excellent husband and father he'd make. Protective, affectionate, devoted.

And here, so far from Spindle Cove and her ambitious mother, almost anything seemed possible.

But then he looked at the sky. "We'd best be on our way home."

On the way home, Charlotte declared herself exhausted. She made a bed for herself in the back of the wagon.

Diana sat on the driver's box beside Aaron. They talked of nothings for the first hour or so, while the sun sank lower in the sky.

Finally, Diana chanced a quick look over her shoulder at the wagon bed. "I think she's asleep."

"Thank God." Aaron transferred the reins to one hand, then used his free arm to draw her close. He tucked her head against his shoulder. "You can rest, too, if you like."

"And waste this precious time with you? Never." She looked up at him. "I liked your sister very much."

"She liked you."

Diana laughed a little. "No, she didn't. She was kind and hospitable, but terribly suspicious of me."

He shook his head in denial.

"Yes, she was. She was suspicious of me because she cares about you. And that's why I liked her." She reached up and touched his newly cropped hair. "I'm glad you have someone looking out for you."

His hand stroked up and down her arm.

"I hope you weren't offended that I didn't tell my own sister the truth."

His hand stopped stroking. "No, I understood it."

"Did you? Perhaps you can explain it to me, then."

She felt him shrug. "No reason to have your family in a lather until you're sure about a thing."

"I suppose you're right."

"There's no rush. We're just getting to know one another."

Were they, really? Diana was so confused. This was more than a casual acquaintance. She was coming to care for him. In truth, she'd begun to care for him some time ago, but every hour they spent together strengthened the attraction.

He wasn't just a well-built body, a handsome face, and a talented kisser. He was a good man, and he deserved to be with someone who could love him unreservedly. He was offering her patience, but she knew she owed it to him to make up her mind. Either accept him for the man he was, or let him find someone else.

It was as though he heard her thoughts.

He glanced at her. "I won't think less of you."

"*I'd* think less of me."

He put space between them, and his voice grew stern. "Don't do this to prove something about yourself, Diana. Not to me, or to your mother, or to anyone. There's no shame in honesty. And there's no romance in glossing over the realities. We could both cite several reasons to let this go."

"You mean realities such as . . . you need a wife who can cook?"

"Or that you need a husband who can move in society."

"Your sister might never accept me," she said.

He nodded and said, in a perfectly serious tone, "Your mother might implode."

She laughed, then laid her head on his shoulder. "Honestly, it's Charlotte. The effect on Charlotte is my greatest concern."

"And that's not something to be brushed aside. If my own sister's future were at risk, I'd be thinking long and hard about it, too."

As they crested another of Sussex's rolling hills, she wondered if she'd ever meet another man who made her feel so free to be honest. And she had the awful, sinking feeling that with all their honesty, they'd just talked themselves out of a future together.

"Aaron, I know it's unrealistic to say the differences won't matter. To say 'Love conquers all.' But if you—"

He shushed her.

Oh, drat. She'd used the word *love*. She'd broken the cardinal rule of female subtleties, as her mother described them. She'd spoken That Word aloud, and he wasn't ready for it.

And *now* it truly was over.

CHAPTER 8

Aaron had never been more reluctant to interrupt a lady, but in this instance, he had no choice.

He slowed the horses to a walk and explained, "There's someone in the road ahead. Stay calm, and let me do the talking."

To the side of the road, a donkey cart appeared to have lost its wheel. The driver of the cart stood in the center of the lane, wearing a patched coat and waving his hat in a plea for assistance.

"Does he need help?" Diana whispered.

"He might be looking for help." *Or he might be looking for trouble.*

Aaron stopped a fair distance from the cart. He reached under the driver's box and retrieved the pistol he kept there. He'd loaded the weapon before setting off from Hastings, and now he was glad of it. This man looked honest enough at a glance—but it never hurt to be cautious.

Patched Coat jammed his hat back on his head and approached their wagon. "Good afternoon, sir. My cartwheel's gone off its axle, and I can't repair it on my own. As you can see, the missus is in a delicate state."

He nodded toward the cart, and behind it Aaron could make out the shadowy form of a woman great with child.

"Can I ask for a moment's assistance, sir? With the two of us, we should have it mended in a trice."

Aaron hesitated. There was a canny glint in the man's eyes and an oily quality in his smile. He didn't like this.

But Diana dug her elbow into his ribs. "She's pregnant. Night will fall before long. We have to help them."

That settled matters. Aaron was obligated now. He couldn't look like a callous, unsympathetic monster in front of the woman who had, just two minutes ago, danced on the verge of professing to love him.

"I'll be right there," he told the man, and he directed the horses as they pulled the wagon aside.

"You stay here," he told Diana in a firm, low voice. He put the pistol in her lap and the reins in her hands. "Chances are, I'll be back in two minutes. But if anything untoward happens, you drive away. If I call to you to drive, you drive away. Do you understand? If there's trouble, I can handle myself. But I can't handle myself *and* protect you and Charlotte."

She nodded. "I understand."

Aaron jumped down from the wagon, and his boots landed in the mud with a squelch. He rued wearing his finest coat now, having stupidly donned it just to impress Diana. The later the hour, the greater the dangers of highway travel grew. Any appearance of riches could put her at risk.

"I do appreciate your help," Patched Coat said, walking

him over to the disabled cart. "This will take no time at all. Big fellow like you? You can lift, and I'll replace the wheel."

Aaron ducked and took a quick peek under the cart. Though the wheel was off the axle, he saw nothing broken or damaged. In fact, the dried mud on the wheel rims suggested this cart hadn't moved in several hours.

"You'll want to remove your coat," the man said. "My missus would be glad to hold it for you."

Of course she would. And she'd be glad to strip the contents from every pocket while she was at it.

Aaron saw exactly what was happening now. This couple had probably been sitting by the road all afternoon, taking that cartwheel off and then flagging down passersby for assistance in "repairing" it. While the unsuspecting travelers performed a good deed, the "missus" would relieve them of their coin.

At least these were petty swindlers, not violent highwaymen. Aaron could get out of this easily enough.

He played along to a point, dutifully lifting the cart so that Patched Coat could fit the wheel back on the axle. Just as he'd probably done four times already today.

Aaron tipped his hat to Mrs. Patched Coat—whose pregnant belly looked a great deal lumpier than any he'd ever seen—and took his leave. "Best of luck to you both."

Find some other unsuspecting fool to gull.

Damn it, the bastard followed him. "Say, I wonder if you could spare a blanket or—"

Aaron stopped in his paces and wheeled on him. "Not another step."

"Why, I didn't mean any—"

Aaron lowered his voice to a threat and loomed over the man. "You will not come one step nearer my wagon. I've helped you with your cart. If you know what's good for you, turn around and walk back."

"Aaron?" Diana called from the wagon. "Is everything all right?"

He lifted his eyebrows at Patched Coat. *You tell me. Are you going to be sensible and turn around, slink back to your donkey cart? Or is this going to get ugly?*

It got ugly. The man pulled a knife.

Aaron took a quick step back, putting himself out of reach.

"That's a fine lady you have there," the man said, gesturing with the gleaming point of his blade. "I'd imagine you work to keep her happy. Surely there's something in your wagon my missus would enjoy."

Without turning his gaze, Aaron lifted his voice. "Diana, drive on. Now."

"I can't," she replied. "I'm not going to leave you here."

"Drive. *Now.*"

When several seconds passed and Diana failed to obey his command, a smile spread across Patched Coat's face. He swiveled the blade back and forth, taunting. "I think she likes me."

Aaron swung on instinct, wanting to knock that smile straight off the bastard's face and grind his nose into the gravel. His punch connected—but so did Patched Coat's blade, slashing through the wool of Aaron's coat sleeve.

They reeled apart from each other and prepared to clash again.

On some level, Aaron registered the fact that he'd been cut. But his mind took the pain and stashed it away for later. He could weather far worse—and he would. He was the human equivalent of an oak tree. If this bastard wanted to bring him down with that puny blade, he'd have to hack at Aaron all night long.

"Diana," he said, keeping his eyes on that glittering, twisting blade. "For the last time, *go*."

Patched Coat began to chuckle. "See now, *my* missus always listens to me." He lifted his voice and called to his wife. "Search the wagon while I hold him here."

A sound stopped them all cold.

The click of a pistol being cocked.

"I don't think so." Diana's voice, as cool and calm as he'd ever heard it. "Step away from him," she told Patched Coat. "Or I will shoot."

Aaron cringed. Damn it all. Why had she refused to drive away? This couldn't end well. If she lost her nerve, she could lose her life. And if she did shoot . . . He knew Diana. Taking a life would weigh heavy on her, even if the act was justified.

"Step away from him now," she repeated, "or I will shoot."

She didn't give a third warning.

Bang.

As the smoke cleared, Patched Coat let out a howl of pain, clutching his right hand in his left. The hand didn't appear to be bleeding, but the knife was gone.

Good Lord. Aaron realized what had happened. She'd

shot the thing clean out of his hand. And the force of the weapon ripping free must have hurt—perhaps broken some of his fingers or his wrist.

Good.

"Jesus," the man whimpered, doubling over and nursing his wounded hand. "That sodding bitch."

Aaron had spent a lifetime staring into red-hot flames. And in that moment, he saw shades of red he'd never dreamed existed. He whipped a back-handed blow across the man's face. Then he grabbed that patched overcoat by the lapels and held the despicable knave close.

"I will rip out your tongue," he growled, "and feed it back to you."

He drove his knee into the blackguard's gut.

He wanted to follow with a crushing punch to the jaw. Then a kick to the ribs. He could have pummeled the bastard into the mud and left him for the carrion birds.

But Diana's voice called to him, dragging him back from the edge of further violence. "Aaron, please. Please, you're bleeding. Let's just go."

Diana knew she'd look back on this half hour and wonder how she'd held herself together. But what mattered now was that she did. Her body and emotions went numb. Some stronger force in her had taken over the moment she'd raised that pistol. All those years of staying calm paid their dividends today. She didn't fret, didn't cry. Her breathing never faltered. She simply did what needed to be done.

She drove the horses a few miles down the road, until they reached a safe place to draw the wagon aside. If she waited any longer, they'd lose all daylight.

She helped Aaron out of his coat and ripped his sleeve apart to expose his wound. Unable to see it well, she took water from their drinking supply and washed the blood away.

A narrow, clean cut, some two inches long. Unless it festered, it wasn't a life-threatening wound—the wool of his coat had served as weak armor—but it was significantly more than a scratch.

"It will need to be stitched," she said dispassionately.

She washed it again, making sure no fibers from his shirt and coat were caught in the wound. Then she rummaged through the goods they'd purchased at the draper's until she found a needle and strong thread.

She was halfway through her third stitch when she thought she felt a drop of rain land on her head. Looking up, she realized it wasn't rain at all but a drop of Aaron's sweat. The poor man. He was shaking, slick with cold perspiration. And here she hadn't offered him anything to help with the pain—not even a scrap of leather to bite down on.

"Go on," he said through gritted teeth. "Finish it."

After three more stitches, she was able to tie the knot off with her teeth. She wrapped a length of white, gauzy fabric about his arm.

"It's a fortunate thing we came from the draper's today and not the millinery," she said dryly.

He stared down at the makeshift bandage. "I'm sorry. This was meant for your costume."

"Never mind the silly play. There's plenty of surplus,

anyhow. I'm just glad I chose to buy needle and thread today, too."

Now that the bandaging was finished, he mopped his face and composed himself. Then asked the question she'd been dreading.

"Why'd you do that? I told you to drive. You were supposed to drive away. Like you promised me."

"I know. But . . ."

"But what?" Oh, he was angry now. His voice shook with emotion, and his hands clenched in iron grips. "You put your life at risk, and Charlotte's, too."

"Aaron, I just couldn't leave you. It was all my fault you stopped to help them. I couldn't simply drive away."

"It's a damned lucky thing you're such a good shot. That was a risky trick, aiming for that knife. If you'd missed . . ."

"I *did* miss." And now the emotion came. Her eyes teared up, and she began to tremble. "I did miss, curse you. My hand was unsteady, and I wasn't braced for the recoil. I wasn't aiming for the stupid knife. I was aiming for him."

He touched her face. "Oh, love."

She made an impatient swipe at her eyes. "And just think—the other day I was debating whether I could kill an eel to keep you. Tonight, when I saw that man lunge with his knife? There was no hesitation. I would have done anything, Aaron. Anything but leave you there alone."

He was silent for a moment. Then he seized her by the arms. His grip was tight, and his voice was all rough edges.

"I need to know," he said. "I need to know, right now, if you're mine. I've been patient for years, and if need be, I can wait years more. I'll do anything in my power to win you, to keep you. But I need to know, this moment, if you'll be mine in the end." His hands moved to bracket her face, uncomfortably tight. His gaze burned into hers. "Tell me."

With every wild beat, her heart thumped against his pendant.

If she was looking for answers, she didn't need to search any further than that.

"Yes," she breathed. "Y—"

Before she could say it twice, his lips were on hers.

And then his hands were everywhere. He thrust them under her cloak, making contact with her shivering body. He cupped her breasts through her frock, slid his hands downward to explore her hips and thighs. The bold possession of his touch stirred her blood. There was nothing of finesse or seduction in his touch. Only claiming. Raw, primal need.

As he ran his tongue along her neck and caught her earlobe in his teeth, he swept one hand down her leg and tossed up the edge of her skirts.

She was visited again by that dizzy, arousing thought from the time before she knew anything of him. From before any of this was possible.

His wrist is as big as my ankle.

Indeed, his fingers encircled her stockinged ankle easily, and she could visualize the corded tendons of his forearm flexing as he stroked higher, higher. Up to her knee, and higher still.

Between her legs, her pulse beat as a sweet, hollow ache.

"Diana," he groaned. "I want to be in you. Deep in the heart of you."

This was madness. It could not happen. Not here, not

now. But she wanted it, too, and the all-consuming nature of her desire was a revelation. What a joy to *want*. To want so fiercely, with all her being, without moderation or reserve.

She was new to this, and the sort of coarse, thrilling words he whispered did not come easily to her lips.

"Yes." At least she could manage that much. "Yes, yes."

He slid his hand higher, over her garter and up. His touch was a brand against her bare, shivering thigh.

She clutched his neck, urging him further. "*Yes.*"

Until Charlotte moaned and stirred in the wagon bed, and they jolted apart.

Her whole body mourned the loss. Her nipples, tight and achy, strained toward him.

"I'd forgotten her." She clapped a hand to her brow.

Aaron chuckled between ragged breaths. "I can't believe she slept through everything."

"She's always been that way. Slept like a stone, ever since she was a baby. I'll be hard-pressed to make her believe any of this tomorrow."

"Then don't try. I think you'd do better to keep it between us."

"But Aaron . . ."

She didn't want to tell Charlotte about the swindler or the fight, but they wouldn't be able to hide their relationship much longer.

"Wait until Thursday," he said. "I want to talk with Lord Payne before we make any plans. I've had my differences with the man, and I didn't care for the way he behaved when he eloped with your sister . . . but I'm determined to do better myself. He's your brother-in-law and the man of the family. I don't need his permission, but I want to speak with him about this—about us—and hear what he has to say. All right?"

She nodded. "All right."

He pressed his brow to hers and caressed her lips with a tender kiss. "There's my girl."

As they kissed, her muzzy thoughts swarmed in two opposite directions, one sublime and one utterly mundane.

The sublime: She was his girl. *His* girl. His *girl*.

The mundane: Now she really had to practice that ridiculous play.

CHAPTER 9

"Ursula was simply too missish to live." The next day, in the parlor of the Queen's Ruby, Charlotte flipped through the booklet and made a face. "It's a miracle no one beheaded her earlier."

"According to the vicar," Diana replied, "even the Church now believes her story is a myth. But I still think we should show some respect."

"Show respect for my nerves," Mama interjected. "Charlotte, pass me the vinaigrette."

"I can't, Mama. It's missing." Charlotte arched a brow at Diana, then slid a glance toward Miss Bertram. "I *told* you there's a pattern," she whispered.

"Missing? Nonsense. It must be here somewhere." Mama rose and began to poke about the room.

"The play," Diana said. "You're supposed to be helping me learn my lines."

Now that Aaron would be in attendance, she actually wanted to do well. Of course, Mama had completely misinterpreted her intentions.

"I'm so glad you're finally making an effort, Diana. Lord Drewe cannot fail to be impressed."

Diana bit back an objection. These few remaining days before Thursday would be her mother's final days to believe she had an obedient, well-intentioned daughter with excellent prospects. She wasn't looking forward to the aftermath, when Mama learned the truth.

Diana opened her booklet to the first page. "Oh, wreck and WOE. My father hath betrothed me to the son of a pagan king. I would sooner DIE than be so defiled."

Charlotte didn't read her part. "I'm finding it hard to sympathize with my role as Cordula," she complained. "If I were friends with this Ursula, I would have shaken some sense into her. I mean, really. So her parents betrothed her to a pagan prince, and she doesn't want to marry him. But instead of just *saying* she doesn't wish to marry him, she asks for a delay and sets sail with eleven thousand of her closest virgin friends, floating about on the ocean for three years."

Diana shrugged. "It sounds rather like a seafaring version of Spindle Cove. Perhaps they amused themselves with theatricals."

"They didn't study celestial navigation, I know that much. Because after three years of drifting, she lands a scant hundred miles away on the shores of France."

Miss Bertram spoke up. "Mr. Evermoore and I have dreamed of taking the Grand Tour. Now that the war's over."

"Oh, of course you have." Charlotte rolled her eyes.

"Go on with Saint Ursula," Diana prompted, anxious for Miss Bertram's feelings.

"This is the best part. Where her army of virgins . . ." Charlotte giggled. "I mean, really. Can you imagine eleven *thousand* virgins, swarming *en masse* over the fields of Gaul? They must have been like a plague of locusts, stripping the fields bare and sucking the rivers dry as they went."

"I suppose that's why it's a myth."

"Right. So the Mythical Virgin Swarm makes it as far as Cologne before running straight into a wall of marauding Huns. Naturally, Ursula refuses to see *them* as husband material. But does she put up any fight? No. Just . . ."

Charlotte drew her finger across her neck and made a grisly slicing sound. "Too missish to live. If she did truly live at all—which history, the Church, and common sense seem to suggest she didn't."

"That doesn't mean we can't learn from her," Diana said.

Exhausted by her fruitless search for the vinaigrette, Mama sank into the nearest chair and snapped open her fan. "You're right, Diana. The moral of the play is clear. Ursula should have married as her parents wished. I'm sure they had good reasons for choosing Meriadoc. He was a prince, and probably quite wealthy."

"No, no." Charlotte strangled the air in a gesture of frustration. "That's not the moral at all. What Ursula *ought* to have done was stand up for herself. If she'd had one good foot-stamping row with her parents and said, 'I'm not going to marry your filthy heathen prince, so there,' she would have saved herself—and her eleven thousand friends—a great deal of trouble."

She fixed Diana with a pointed gaze.

Diana wasn't sure what her sister was getting at. But it made her uncomfortable. Had Charlotte somehow guessed at her relationship with Aaron?

"You are right, Miss Charlotte." Miss Bertram shot to her feet. "I'm going to write to my parents this instant and tell them I cannot be parted from Mr. Evermoore. No matter how they disapprove."

As Miss Bertram stormed from the room, Charlotte grumbled, "At least someone is convinced."

"Can we just rehearse?" Diana asked.

"Yes, indeed!" Mama said. "Diana must learn her lines by heart. You can be assured that Lord Drewe will know his. How many scenes do you have with him, Diana? Is there a kiss?"

Diana threw down the booklet in exasperation. "Ursula dies a virgin, Mother. It's the whole point of the play. There is no marriage. No kiss."

What would Mama say if she knew Diana had kissed Aaron three times now?

Charlotte was right. Diana wanted to respect Aaron's wishes about speaking with her brother-in-law first, but that didn't mean she had to keep up this farce regarding Lord Drewe.

"Mama, I am not going to marry Lord Drewe. He hasn't asked. He isn't likely to ask. And even if he did ask, I would refuse him."

Charlotte pumped her fists in a silent cheer.

Her mother pressed a hand to her heart. She blinked rapidly. Diana began to wonder if she should have saved this speech until after they'd located the missing vinaigrette.

When at last Mama spoke, it was quietly. "I am so proud of you, Diana."

"You . . . you are?"

"Yes. I am proud of you, my dear. And I have felt the same in my own heart, but been reluctant to say it. As long as you've waited to marry, there should be no compromise."

Diana was stunned speechless. If she'd known it would be this easy, she would have initiated this discussion years ago.

"You are right," Mama went on. "You cannot marry the Marquess of Drewe. We must hold out for a duke."

Oh, Lord.

Across from her, Charlotte made the throat-slicing slash and collapsed on the divan.

Since the sky's war on Spindle Cove seemed to be in a temporary cease-fire, Aaron found himself inordinately busy at the forge. Farmers were making use of the break in the rain to shoe their horses and get their hoes, harrows, and plowshares in working order.

Of course, this flurry of business would happen on precisely the few days Aaron wished to have the smithy to himself. He was finding it difficult to steal daylight to work on Diana's ring. Instead, he worked at the mold by night, lighting unprecedented numbers of candles at his kitchen table.

At last he was finished, and he managed to scrape up an hour to cast the thing. He heated the gold in a crucible and poured it into the mold. When it cooled, he held it up for inspection.

Not bad. But not good enough. He'd tweak the mold and melt it down again.

As he lowered the ring, he caught a flash of golden-blond hair headed straight up his lane. At any other time, he would have been thrilled to see her, but now?

Devil. Blast. Shite.

Hastily, he shoved the unfinished ring and all accompanying evidence aside, tossing a rag over the lot of it just as she entered the forge.

And after all that effort—the golden-blond hair didn't belong to Diana at all.

"Miss Charlotte," he said, wiping the sweat from his brow. "This is a surprise. What can I do for you?"

She made herself at home, settling on a stool. "We've had a mysterious rash of thefts at the Queen's Ruby. Diana's thimble. Mrs. Nichols's ink bottle. Mama's lorgnette, my vinaigrette, and sundry loose coins."

"That wouldn't seem to add up to much."

"It adds up to a pattern," she said. "A mystery. I've appointed myself investigator, and I'm making interviews. Do you mind if I ask you a few questions?"

"Not at all."

She took out a notebook and pencil. "Now, then. Mr. Dawes, do you have any idea who might have taken the missing objects?"

"I can't say that I do, Miss Charlotte."

"Has anyone brought any suspicious items to the forge?"

"No."

"Very good. Just one last question." She lowered her notebook. "Do you mean to marry my sister?"

Aaron looked up at her, startled. "What does that have to do with missing trinkets?"

"Nothing." Miss Charlotte shrugged. "I'm just proving my powers of deduction, that's all. I may not know who's been filching things around the rooming house—yet—but I know there's something between you and Diana."

"Did she tell you?"

"No."

"Then when . . . ?" God. He hoped she hadn't witnessed them on the way home from Hastings.

"I've known for more than a year! After I missed the signs when Minerva eloped, I made a commitment to observation. I've long known she fancied you." Her head tilted. "If you do mean to propose, you will have to confront my mother."

"I . . ." Aaron didn't know how to refute the idea. So he didn't. "I know I will."

"Do you have a plan of attack?"

"Attack?"

Charlotte's bow-shaped mouth quirked. "This is my mother you're dealing with. She's a dragon. Arm yourself. Gird your loins. Gather your courage and your best steel. And yes, formulate a plan of attack."

Aaron just shook his head. He knew the matron would be surprised and displeased, to say the least, but he didn't want to see Mrs. Highwood as an enemy. He was usually *good* with mothers and sisters.

Miss Charlotte brought out a fan from her reticule, snapped it open, and began to work it vigorously. "Here. Let's play a scene."

"I know you ladies enjoy your theatricals, but I don't count acting among my talents."

"But you don't have to act. You're you. And I'm my mother." She adopted a high, screeching tone. "My Diana, marry a *blacksmith?* Of all the horrid, unthinkable notions. She will marry a lord. If not a duke! She is the beauty of the family, as everyone knows."

Aaron sighed under his breath. He tried to exercise patience with the matriarch of the Highwood family, knowing most of her excesses were born out of a desire for her daughters' well-being. But he heartily disliked the way she compared the Highwood sisters against each other.

"Miss Charlotte, you are a very pretty girl. Well on the way to becoming a beauty in your own right."

She made a face. "I wasn't fishing for compliments. I'm pretty enough, but Diana *is* the beauty of the family. Just like Minerva's the brains of the family."

"And what are you?"

She smiled proudly. "The spirit, of course. Now come along." She fluttered the fan. "Argue back."

Aaron wiped his hands on a rag and sat down across from her. "Here's the thing of it, Miss Charlotte. If your sister married me, it would affect your whole family."

"Naturally. Diana will live here, and Min and I should always have a reason to visit Spindle Cove. That will make all three of us happy."

"You know that's not what I mean. Your own prospects. You're going to have your season in London soon. And I suspect you want that excitement, even if it didn't suit your sisters. If Miss Diana marries this far beneath her station"—he quelled Charlotte's objection with a hand gesture—"there's bound to be gossip. Fewer invitations, fewer suitors . . ."

He could tell his words were sinking in. She shifted uncomfortably on her stool.

"Listen, Mr. Dawes. I don't think you've understood. *I'm* meant to be my mother in this scene we're playing, and you're stealing all her lines."

He chuckled. "Let's just say I've realized something. If there's a member of the Highwood family I must approach for permission, it's not your mother. It's you."

She sat tall. "Well. Don't *I* feel important."

"You are important. I know Diana wouldn't like to see you hurt."

"I don't like to see Diana hurt, either, Mr. Dawes. And yet I've watched her hurting ever since I could remember. I've held her hand through horrid, endless minutes when she struggled to simply breathe. While I would run and climb and play, she was always kept indoors. I was young then, but I've grown up now. I won't have her penned up for another two years just so I can dance and make merry in Town." Her gaze lifted to his. "I want, very much, to see my sister happy. If it's my blessing you need, you have it."

He nodded slowly. "Very well, then. But you may regret this when the London bucks come chasing after you and your brother-in-law threatens them with a red-hot poker."

She laughed. "You wouldn't."

"I would. Ask my own sisters." He rubbed his face. "But I'm getting ahead of myself. I haven't properly proposed."

Charlotte hopped down from the stool and reached for her cloak. "That's one answer you needn't worry about."

CHAPTER 10

On Thursday, Aaron took his time getting ready.

After a thorough dousing at the pump, he shaved as close as he could manage. Tonight had to be perfect. He thought of the women making ready at the Queen's Ruby. All the ladies flitting and hurrying about in their underthings, trading ribbons and hairpins.

Diana, rolling a pale silk stocking up her leg.

That mental picture earned him a nick beneath his jaw. He examined the red line in the tiny looking glass and swore. So much for perfect.

He donned a new starched shirt, holding the collar as wide as possible so as not to spot the thing with blood. As he wrestled with his cuffs, he tried not to remind himself that a proper gentleman would have a valet to help him with these things. Last came his cleaned and mended brown coat—still the best he had, even after the roadside brawl.

Good thing he didn't possess a full-length mirror, or it surely would have reflected a picture of discouragement.

What sort of miracle was he trying to work, anyhow? She

knew him. It wasn't as though he could fool her into thinking he was something loftier than a village blacksmith.

He started out the door and was halfway through saddling his horse when he stopped short.

In his agitation, he'd nearly forgotten the ring. Of all the things to forget. It was the one item he had to recommend him, after all.

He opened the small lockbox in his bedchamber and pulled it out, letting it glitter on the palm of his hand. He'd used gold—it suited her golden hair, and it was the finest. The band was adorned with leaves, with a small center ruby set amid diamond petals. Even if she wouldn't marry him, he wanted her to have this. It was the best of him, and the best he knew how to offer.

His guts were in knots. This was absurd.

He was who he was. She would have him, or she wouldn't. After tonight, he'd know.

"Mr. Dawes!" The voice came from the smithy. "Mr. Dawes!"

Aaron slipped the ring in his breast pocket before walking out and around to the front. He found Cora Maidstone, the daughter of one of the local farmers. From the state of her flushed cheeks and muddied hem, he surmised she'd run all the way here.

"What is it?" he asked.

"It's my father," she said, breathless. "Our mare's been tetchy lately, and she rolled him. Broke his leg. Bad."

Aaron passed a hand over his face. The Maidstone family, like so many of the farming families, lived year to year. This was planting season, and his sons weren't old enough yet to take on the plowing. If that leg didn't heal properly—or didn't heal at all—the whole family could starve.

"Please," she said. "He's hurting something fierce."

"Of course. Give me a moment."

He strode back into his cottage, shrugged out of his coat, and slung it on a hook. He gathered an apron and the kit of laudanum, bandages, and such that Lady Rycliff had given him to keep on hand for bonesettings.

Last, he put that gold and ruby ring back into the lockbox and shut it tight. There'd be no theatricals or parties for him today. He had work to do, and there was no way around it.

He was who he was.

As for whether Diana would have him—he could only pray she'd give him another chance to ask.

Several fatiguing, bloody hours later, Aaron rode through the village on his way back. It was out of his way, but something wouldn't let him go home until he passed by the cheerful façade of the Queen's Ruby, with its begonia-stuffed window boxes and green shutters.

He stared up at the window he knew to be hers. Dark, like all the others. Ambervale was a few hours' distance, and it would likely be almost dawn before the ladies returned home. Aaron hated to imagine what Diana would think of him, promising to attend and then failing to appear. He should have thought to send word at least, but there hadn't been time.

Well, there was nothing for it but to apologize tomorrow.

He nudged his horse and turned down the lane that led home. As he neared the cottage, he saw a weak light burning from within. Strange. In his hurry, he must have neglected to extinguish his lamp before leaving.

He took his time putting up the horse, making sure the mare had water, feed, and a good brushing down. Then Aaron had a glance at himself and grimaced. The fresh new shirt he'd worn for the occasion was spattered with blood. He gave a grim chuckle, thinking of how he'd been so careful not to mar it with the smallest drop from his shaving accident.

Right there by the pump, he yanked the shirt loose of his waistband, pulled it over his head, and cast it into a bucket of water to soak. No use bringing the thing inside. Then he doused his own head, torso, and hands, washing away all the evidence of that evening's miserable, bloody work. Finally, he stood erect, pushed the water from his face and hair, and went into the cottage.

She was there. Sitting at his table, head rested on her stacked arms.

"Diana?"

She woke with a start, her eyes wide and unfocused until they settled on him. "Aaron. You're here."

"I'm here. And you're here. What about Ambervale?"

"I told everyone I had a miserable headache and begged Miss Bertram to read my part. I didn't go."

"Why not?"

"We heard from one of the inn's girls about Mr. Maidstone's accident. And I knew you'd be called to help. How is he?"

Aaron sighed and rubbed his jaw. "He'll live. His leg's set as best I could manage. It was a bad break, and it will take months to heal. But if he gives it time, it should heal cleanly."

"That's a relief."

"Seeing your face is a relief. I worried what you'd think when I didn't come."

"I wanted to come help you, but I decided I'd only be in the way. But I knew you'd be famished once it was over. And perhaps needing some company, too." She averted her gaze, and her eyelashes fluttered.

It suddenly occurred to him that he was standing before her shirtless. And that she'd noticed. Her wide-eyed, sleepy gaze wandered over every damp contour of his arms and chest. But she sat between him and the bedchamber, where all his other clothing hung. Improper as it was for her to see him half dressed, he couldn't clothe himself without drawing imprudently near . . . so he simply did nothing at all.

Well, he did clear his throat.

Her gaze snapped up to his face.

She pushed to her feet. "I brought over some dinner." As she indicated the covered dishes on the table, her mouth pulled to the side in a self-deprecating smile. "Don't worry, I didn't cook it myself. It's just odds and ends from the Queen's Ruby kitchen."

He didn't know what to say—the fact that she'd known, that she'd given up the evening's amusement to be with him. Her thoughtfulness wasn't any sort of surprise, but still . . . His heart insisted it meant so much more.

And she was so damned beautiful. Whatever gown or costume she'd been meant to wear for the theatrical, it had been hung away again. She wore one of her simplest, everyday frocks. But her hair was still put up in careful coils and ringlets, like an artifact of the revelry she'd forfeited tonight.

He drew close and caught a lock of that lovely golden hair, wrapping it around his finger. "I'm sorry you missed the outing."

"I'm not sorry." She swallowed hard. "I mean, it couldn't be helped."

"Of course it could. You needn't have stayed home. I know you were looking forward to seeing your sister and your friends."

"I was mostly looking forward to you."

He skimmed a touch down her cheek, overwhelmed—and at a loss to imagine what he'd ever done to deserve those words. To deserve this woman.

"Are you hungry?" she asked.

He nodded. "Yes."

"Well, then. Perhaps I should get some plates and—"

He pulled her into a kiss.

He was hungry, yes. Hungry for her. His soul was starved for just this.

He'd been returning to this house, to this very room, every night of his life. But this was the first time in a long time it felt like truly coming home.

She was soft and welcoming. She smelled so damned good.

He cinched an arm tight about her slender waist, trapping her arms against his bare chest. Her fingertips explored, stroked, caressed. And then slowly slid upward, until she wreathed her arms about his neck and held him tight.

They kissed and touched. He put a hand to her breast, kneading and shaping. She sighed, arching into his caress. Begging for more. He pulled her up against him, insinuating one thigh between her legs. She rewarded him with a husky moan and a deep, demanding kiss.

It was night. They were alone, and no one was going to interrupt them. In the other room, a bed beckoned. He was already half undressed. It didn't take a fortune-teller to see where this was going.

He murmured, "If you don't want this . . ."

He couldn't even complete the sentence. *Want this*, he silently pleaded. *Want this—want me, want this life we could share—as much as I want you.*

"I want this," she whispered. Her hips rolled against the firm slope of his thigh, sending streaks of raw lust through him. "Aaron, I . . . I want it so much."

"I had a question I meant to ask you tonight."

"I know." Her blue eyes tipped up, meeting his gaze directly. "I came here to say yes."

He didn't even make a reply.

Because there was nothing left to say. If she wanted him, he was hers. Tonight, tomorrow, always.

He swept her off her feet and into his arms. Her little shriek of laughter delighted him. He'd been wanting to do that since the first.

As he laid her down, he wished he had a better bed. A plusher mattress on a hardwood frame. Softer linens and quilts. But none of these misgivings were enough to dampen his lust. Not in the least. As he slid a hand under her skirts, his cock felt like a rod of steel in his trousers. He hadn't known this pitch of erotic desperation since he was a youth of sixteen.

Nevertheless, he resolved to take things slowly. He knew

her pleasure must come first, or it wasn't likely to happen at all.

As he fumbled with the hooks down the back of her frock, nerves swarmed him like agitated bees. He hoped to God he *could* make this good for her. He'd never bedded a virgin. Hell, he hadn't been with any woman in quite some time.

He'd spent his youth working too hard to chase after girls. Eventually, a friendly widow in the next village had taken him in hand—and taken him in plenty of other ways, teaching him the lay of the female landscape. They'd had an easy friendship, but he'd broken it off when he'd started courting the schoolteacher. And after the schoolteacher had dropped him, he'd wasted a few evenings carousing in town to soothe his wounded pride.

And that was the sum of it.

Here he was, a virile, red-blooded man of seven-and-twenty, and he could count his lovers on one hand. His hand, of course, being the most familiar lover of all.

Diana's hands were a welcome improvement. They were soft. So soft, and so wonderfully curious. As he tugged down the bodice of her frock, she skimmed inquisitive touches up his arms, across his shoulders, down the planes of his chest. Awakening his every nerve and whipping his heartbeat to a gallop.

He removed her frock and carefully laid it aside, leaving her clad in a sweet, simple chemise and stockings. Silk stockings, from the feel of them. He ran a hand up her calf, imagining the feel of her legs locked around his waist. Just the thought made him groan with anticipated pleasure.

"You like them?" she asked. "They're my best."

"I'm surprised you didn't change when you decided to stay home." He touched the edge of her ribbon garter, but he didn't untie it.

She gave him a kittenish smile. "Oh, I did change. I put these on for you."

Lust streaked through him, nearly cleaving him in half. Neither of them were even naked yet, and he was already primed to spill.

"God, I love you." It wasn't the eloquent confession she deserved. But *something* in him had to erupt, and words seemed the safest quantity.

She laughed and kissed him. As their tongues danced, he sent his fingers to undo the tiny buttons queued down the front of her shift. There were hundreds, it seemed.

At last he'd loosened enough of those buttons to draw the edges apart and slide his hand inside.

Sweet heaven.

He was a smith. He worked with hard, solid, unforgiving materials all day long. But this . . . Ah, this was softness.

Nothing could compare to the sensation of her breast filling his hand. Nothing. He stroked, lifted, kneaded, teased. He couldn't get enough of touching her.

He dropped his head, trailing kisses down her neck and breastbone, wrenching the edges of her shift aside until the rest of the buttons popped free. He paused just long enough to register the color of her nipple—a pale, tawny pink—before taking it in his mouth.

She gasped and sighed. Her fingers wove tight in his hair.

With one hand, he raised the hem of her shift, taking time to savor the glide of silk before seeking the delicate folds of her sex. She parted her thighs with an eager innocence, but from there progress slowed.

She was so small, so tight. Just working a single finger into her sheath took ages. And as men went, Aaron knew he was on the larger side. His past lovers had been glad of it. But in this situation . . .

Gathering all of his patience, he stroked that single finger in and out, all the while suckling her breasts and rubbing the heel of his palm against her pearl. Her erotic, breathy moans encouraged him, as did the increasing heat.

But when he tried to add a second finger, she tensed all over.

He withdrew his touch at once, cursing his rough workman's hands. He drew her shift down, covering her to the knees.

"I don't want you to fear this. And I can't bear to cause you any pain." The words were hell to get out, but he knew he must. "Perhaps we should wait."

Her blue eyes glistened with emotion. Her kiss-swollen lips parted, spilling the most un-Diana-Highwood words he'd ever heard her speak.

"Like the devil we should."

Diana savored his blank look of surprise.

He wasn't accustomed to such language from her. She wasn't accustomed to *using* such language. But on this point, propriety could go hang. She wouldn't leave any room for ambiguity.

This needed to happen. Tonight.

She struggled up on her elbow, turning onto her side so that they faced one another on the bed. "Aaron, I was attracted to you from our first acquaintance. Infatuated with you not long after. But I fell in love with you because you put the reins in my hands. You trusted me to know my own mind, and you gave me the courage to follow my heart. That's the reason I'm here tonight."

He stroked her arm. "If you tell me you're certain . . ."

"I'm certain. All my life I've kept a safe distance from my own emotions. No longer. If fear is part of this, then I want to feel fear. Pain, as well. And joy and anxiousness and need and pleasure and . . . and everything, all at once. I want to experience all of it, and I want it with you."

A finality settled on his features. "Then you'll have it."

Yes. Feeling triumphant, Diana relaxed back onto the bed, stretching her limbs in a sinuous plea for his touch.

He caressed her with his eyes first, sweeping a determined gaze over her body.

"Do you understand pleasure?" His hand eased between her thighs, cupping her sex through her shift. "This will go much easier if you reach climax first."

He asked her the question so baldly. Even hopefully. She answered with the truth. "Yes."

"Good." His voice was a low, dark thrum. "Good."

She arched her back, pushing into his touch.

"Yes," he said. "Show me what pleases you."

Her boldness faltered. There was admission, and then there was demonstration. But she pressed her eyes closed, gathered her courage, and reached down to cover his hand with her own.

She didn't guide him under her shift but pressed his fingers to her flesh through the muslin, working the smooth, strong friction in just the right place.

Once he'd established a rhythm, she relaxed her grip and melted against the mattress. He kissed her breasts, her ears, her neck. His skillful touch and talented mouth were arousing sensations different from any she'd ever experienced. This wasn't a moment's gratification in the bathing tub. This was an ocean. A vast sea of pleasure, swirling around her, lifting and tossing her in ways she couldn't control.

The only course was surrender.

Her breath grew ragged, and she writhed, uneasy, on the bed. He fitted his mouth over her nipple and drew hard, teasing the tip with wicked lashings of his tongue. The joy was so acute. A delicious urgency bloomed and spread through her whole body. She dug her heel into the mattress, rolling her hips to meet his touch.

"Yes," he whispered, abandoning one nipple just long enough to catch the other. "That's it."

He removed his hand from between her legs. She whimpered at the deprivation, until he moved to cover her with the full length of his body. He still wore his trousers, but the sheer heat and weight of him were sensual gifts. The hair on his chest teased her sensitized nipples. His hips nudged her thighs wide, and then the smooth, thick column of his trapped erection settled snug in her cleft.

Yes. This. The firm, perfect pressure was just what she'd needed. He moved against her in a slow, tantalizing rhythm, and she rode his motions.

"Aaron." She clutched at his shoulders and neck, holding on for her life as the pleasure tugged her in ten different directions.

And then it all came together in one brilliant, shattering wave of joy.

No sooner had her climax ebbed than he was backing away, yanking at the buttons on his trousers and cursing his boots as he stripped to his skin. He pushed her shift to the waist, gazing boldly on her most intimate places. But before she could think to squirm or shy from him, he'd settled atop her again.

His thighs were hard against hers, and covered with hair, much like his chest. The smooth, broad crown of his manhood prodded at her core.

He groaned. "I . . . I don't know that I can wait much longer."

"I think we've both waited long enough."

His hips flexed, and he pushed forward.

Inside her.

She buried her face in his neck, determined not to cry out.

He cursed. "It will be better next time. I promise."

It hurt. It hurt fiercely—so much that only the tang of blood made her aware that she'd bitten her lip.

It will be better next time, she consoled herself as a series of slow, persistent thrusts took him deeper. Brought them closer. *It will be better next time.*

But once she'd reconciled herself to the promise of *Next time. . .*

This time started to feel rather good.

She wouldn't climax again. That wasn't even a question.

But the sublime feeling of being needed, desired, *loved* with such vigor and passion . . . this was a new, intoxicating pleasure all its own. She held him tight, loving the feel of his flexing, straining muscles as he buried his length deep at the heart of her, then strove to go deeper still.

His motions quickened, grew less elegant and controlled. Her breathing was labored in a way that would have alarmed her in her youth.

Not anymore.

He kept his weight balanced on his elbows, and she curled her neck to kiss him on the chest, the neck . . . anywhere she could reach. She ran her tongue along his collarbone, feeling brazen and seductive.

With a strangled groan, he slid one hand to her backside, holding her tight for a final barrage of thrusts. His face twisted into a mask of torturous pleasure.

At last, he slumped atop her, growling and shuddering with the force of completion. Filling her deep.

He remained inside her, slowly softening as his labored breath caressed her neck.

He was quiet and still for a long, long time. Because they'd earned this, too—this refuge in each other. In all her life, she'd never felt so perfectly loved and safe.

"You can't know," he finally whispered into her hair. "You can't know how long I've wanted this."

She turned her head, seeking his kiss. "I think I have some idea."

CHAPTER 11

Diana slept late the next morning. She assumed everyone in the Queen's Ruby would.

She'd been back safe in her own bed for less than an hour before the carriages had rattled into the village center. The girls had come tromping up the stairs, giggling and whispering to one another. It would seem they'd managed to have their fun without Diana's help. She was glad of it. Part of her had been tempted to come out of her room and ask for all the details. She wanted to hear all the news of Kate and Minerva.

But she'd decided there would be time enough for those questions in the morning. Her night with Aaron had left her blissfully sapped of strength, and she *was* supposed to be ill.

So when Charlotte had opened her door a crack and whispered a cautious "Diana?"she hadn't answered but pretended to be asleep. And then she'd fallen asleep in truth.

She slept hard. Her body had earned it.

When she woke, she could hear the sounds of breakfast. Her chamber was situated directly above the dining room, and she knew well that distant murmur of porcelain and cutlery, delivered on air scented of buttered toast.

She rose, washed, and dressed in her favorite frock, then clattered down the stairs.

No, not clattered.

She *floated* down the stairs.

She was in *love*. She was getting *married*. She would have a sweet little cottage in this village she'd come to think of as home, and she and Aaron would build a life and a family together. It might not be the future her mother had planned, but it was more happiness than Diana had ever dreamed she'd grasp.

And by the end of today, everyone would know the truth.

In the corridor, she slowed, intrigued by the sounds coming from the dining room.

"She's coming," someone whispered.

A roar of shushing ensued. There was a rattle of panicked flatware.

Then Diana turned the corner and entered the dining room, and everyone fell completely, eerily silent.

"My goodness," she said. "What is it? What's wrong?"

One of the girls set down her spoon. "See, I *told* you she'd know nothing about it. It couldn't have been her."

"Hush, Fanny." Miss Price cleared her throat and looked Diana over. "You look quite well this morning, Miss Highwood. One would never know you were ill last night."

"Thank you." Diana spoke slowly, not liking the suspicious tone in Miss Price's voice. "I am feeling much improved."

All of the ladies regarded her warily, even as they sent speaking glances to each other.

Diana's heart began to pound.

Oh, Lord. They *knew*. They all knew. Someone had noticed her sneaking out to see Aaron. Or sneaking back in afterward.

"I don't believe it of her," one girl whispered.

"But it couldn't have been anyone else," another replied.

"It's probably a compulsion. I've heard of it happening with some girls. They know it's wrong, but they can't help themselves."

A compulsion?

No, no, no. Diana wasn't suffering any compulsion. She was in *love*. She was *floating*. That's what she'd wanted everyone to see today. Not sordidness.

Instead, they all looked at her sideways and whispered behind their hands.

This was ruination, she realized. Her twenty-three years of delicate refinement didn't matter anymore. Everyone stared at her with revulsion and fear in their eyes. As though her pretty blue frock had been soiled with soot—and if they came too close, it might stain them, too.

She felt truly ill now. What would they think of her? What would this mean for Charlotte?

One thing was certain—their image of the perfect Miss Highwood was now irretrievably shattered.

Miss Price elbowed her neighbor. "Do it. Someone has to ask."

"I'll do it. I'm the landlady. It should be me." Dear old Mrs. Nichols rose from her seat and clasped her hands together in an attitude of prayer. "Diana, dear," she began gently. "Did you have anything to tell us? Anything at all, about last night?"

The rain was back. With a vengeance.

Aaron didn't know what to do with himself. All the Queen's Ruby ladies would surely be sleeping in today, Diana included. He couldn't go call on her until late afternoon, and there wasn't much sense braving this downpour to go anywhere else. He'd looked in on Mr. Maidstone early that morning, after walking Diana back to the rooming house.

He decided to start on a wrought-iron gate for the front garden. He'd long been planning to replace the humble wooden one. He'd just never found the time.

Today, he had all the time he wished.

He built a roaring fire in the forge and took out a length of squared stock. To make spiraling balusters for the gate, he needed to heat the iron to a glowing yellow, crank furiously to secure it in a table vise, grasp the end of the rod with tongs, then twist the metal in as many rotations as he could manage before it cooled.

Then repeat the whole business again. And again.

It was hard, sweaty work—and just the distraction he needed today.

He'd been at it for an hour or two when he saw a figure hurrying up the lane. Who would come out in this weather? He hoped it wasn't the Maidstone girl again, come to tell him her father had taken a turn for the worse.

But when the door burst open, in came Diana.

She removed her cloak and hung it on a peg near the door, then played stork by standing on one foot, then the other, tugging off the canvas gaiters covering her shoes.

Aaron merely stood and stared, letting his rod of twisted iron go cool in the vise. "You shouldn't be out in this weather. You'll catch cold."

Perhaps he should have greeted her with *Good day*, or *What a pleasant surprise*, or *Did I tell you last night that I love you to the depths of my soul?* But he couldn't be bothered with pleasantries now. She'd pledged herself to him, always. He wanted "always" to be a long, long time.

"I just needed to see you. To talk to you. It couldn't wait." She hurried toward him.

"Stop," he said.

She stopped, taken aback.

He cursed his thoughtlessness again. "Sorry. I didn't mean to bark at you. But have a care for your hem and slippers."

He nodded at the ground.

She'd crossed from the paved half of the smithy and trod straight onto the cinders, dragging her damp flounce through the packed soot. That sort of soil was near impossible to clean. Anyone who saw it would know where she'd been.

"It doesn't matter," she said. "I'm cold. I want to be nearer the fire. And you."

"Then put your hands on my shoulders." When she complied, he slid a forearm under her hips and lifted, boosting her to sit on the anvil. He kept his hand clenched and out of the way, to keep from mussing her frock.

But once he had here there, sitting sweetly on his anvil . . .

By God, he wanted to muss her all over.

Five minutes ago, he would have sworn there was no sight on earth more enticing than Miss Diana Highwood in her china-blue frock.

But he was wrong.

There *was* a sight more enticing. It was Miss Diana Highwood in her china-blue frock, damp with rain.

The cloak had protected her from the worst of it, but enough of the weather had seeped through that her bodice might as well have been a coat of paint. Her nipples were hard and perfectly outlined.

Her legs dangled above the cinder floor. He caught a glimpse of her white-clad ankles. No silk stockings today, just sensible wool. He still found them arousing as hell.

"I wasn't expecting you." He wiped his brow with his sleeve, then showed her his blackened hands. "Sit here by the forge. I'll go wash up, find a fresh shirt, build a fire in the cottage. Then I can warm you properly."

She reached for him. "No, stay. Stay with me."

"If you like."

Frowning, he studied her, trying to decide whether her shivering was due to the damp weather or a fragile emotional state. Either way, he didn't like feeling unable to help her.

He couldn't warm her with his hands. But hands weren't the only parts he had.

"Your fingers must be freezing," he said, glancing down at her balled fists.

She nodded.

She wore those knitted handwarmers that seemed popular with all the ladies this spring. Fingerless gloves, he'd heard them called. In weather like this, "fingerless" struck him as tantamount to "useless," but he didn't pretend to understand ladies' fashions.

He untied his leather apron and cast it aside. Then he jerked his homespun shirt free of his waistband and lifted it in invitation. "Put them here."

She pressed her chilled hands flat to his torso. Their coolness gave him a jolt.

"Goodness," she said. "You're like a furnace."

Love, you have no idea.

To be sure, her hands were cold. But her cold fingertips had less chance of dampening his lust than ten snowflakes falling on a bonfire.

His whole body was aflame with desire for her. Had been since long before she'd burst through the door. All he'd been able to think of since last night was her naked body under his. Her sweet touch against his bared skin.

Bending his head, he kissed the pink back to her lips, then her cheeks. He nuzzled the frosty snub of her nose. Licked a stray raindrop from her brow.

"That's better," she said.

"I'm just getting started." He pressed a kiss to her neck. "But you had something to talk about?"

"It can wait."

"Good." He trailed kisses lower. "Good."

Her fingers slid around his rib cage, spreading over the planes of his back, drawing him close. Instinctively, he moved to reciprocate and embrace her, too—but he remembered himself just in time to keep from smearing her frock with soot. Instead, he let his hands drop, and he gripped either end of the anvil.

Her neckline thwarted him. When damp, the muslin had no give. So he dropped his head lower, nuzzling her breasts through her bodice.

She sighed and moved against him, seeking more contact.

He knew she wanted more. Needed more. And he knew how to give it to her, too. He just wasn't sure she was ready to receive it.

No way to find out but to try.

He sank to his knees, ducked his head, and burrowed under her skirts.

She went completely still. Not a muscle moved, but he could hear her breathing. Her breath came from a low place, deep in her belly. Husky and yearning.

She didn't tell him to stop.

He nibbled his way up the stocking-clad slope of her calf and knee, nosing his way through the tunnel of petticoats. When he reached her ribbon garter, he knew paradise was close. He laid his tongue to the bare silk of her inner thigh, then swept boldly upward. As he moved higher, his broad shoulders pushed her legs apart.

Her thigh gave a sweet quiver against his mouth.

He found her center, nestled close, and parted her with his tongue.

She sucked in her breath.

He paused, giving her time to adjust or object if she wished—and he drew a deep inhalation of his own. He breathed the scents of spring rain, and muslin pressed with a hot iron, and her intoxicating feminine essence. So pure, so sensual. It made him wild.

He lapped at her, thirsty for more.

It wasn't long before she surrendered to the pleasure, relaxing into his kiss. He explored gently, tenderly, learning what pleased her and what didn't. He would have loved to bring her to climax this way. But when she tugged at his shoulders in a silent plea for him to rise, he couldn't find any strength to object.

With his teeth, he dragged her skirts to her waist, and he wedged his hips between her spread legs, grinding his buckskin-trapped erection against her aroused flesh.

This was so good.

And so wrong.

A flicker of doubt chased down his spine. It was the middle of the day. Pouring rain outside, yes, but someone *could* come in at any moment. Someone from the rooming house *might* be looking for her.

Were they really going to do this?

Her slender legs locked around his waist. The heel of her slipper dug into his flank—like a spur, prodding his inner beast.

Oh, yes. They were going to do this.

He tightened his grip on the pointed ends of the anvil, bracketing her hips. "You'll have to take it from here."

She reached between them and worked the closures of his trousers, slipping each button free with small, sure fingers. Then those same fingers reached inside and found his straining cock, drawing him out and guiding him to her core.

She was wet and ready. A low groan eased from his chest as he slid deep.

Sweet . . . holy . . . damn.

How many nights had he taken himself in hand and imagined just this scene? Perfect, refined, delicate Diana High-wood propped on his anvil, milk-white thighs spread wide. Panting for him. Her back arched in pleasure, her breasts overflowing her bodice as he took her, pounding a forged-iron erection into her willing heat, again and again and again. She'd always been his favorite erotic fantasy.

But the reality? The reality surpassed his every imagining.

He could never have pictured it like this. The sounds of rain sheeting down, battering the smithy roof. The small, private clouds of their mingled breath. The scent of laundered muslin mingling with raw, animal lust. And God, the feel of her. Her velvet heat hugging his cock. So tight. The sweet vise of her legs locked over his hips. The delicious bite of her fingernails on his neck.

I want this, too, her body told him. *I want this, I want you. I want more, more, more.*

With a low growl, he tightened his grip on the anvil and redoubled his pace. He would give her more. He would give her everything.

"Aaron." Her hands fisted in the fabric of his shirt. "Aaron, wait."

He froze, breath heaving in his chest. Damn. She'd come to her senses, realized she was a gentlewoman being crudely tupped on the anvil in a village smithy. Bloody hell. He was a rutting bastard.

Maybe he could apologize. Make it up to her by carrying her to the cottage and his bed.

Or maybe she'd just leave. Forever.

"I . . ." He didn't know what to say or do. He just hoped she didn't weep.

She looked up at him with sultry, heavy-lidded eyes. "Touch me," she said huskily. "Get me dirty. I don't mind."

Sweet . . . holy . . . damn.

Outside of muttering his way through Sunday service, Aaron had not voiced a conscious prayer in more than ten years. He supposed it wouldn't help his chances in the hereafter if he returned to the fold with *Saints preserve me from premature ejaculation.* No matter how sincerely uttered.

Instead, he gritted his teeth and slowed his thrusts to a languid roll. She held fast to his neck but relaxed her arms, so that she hung pendulous beneath him, affording them both the space to watch.

She looked on, wide-eyed and breathless, as he slid one hand to cup her breast. Her body arched into his touch. His thumb made a dark, rude streak over the pale muslin. Marking her.

She gave a sharp cry of pleasure, and her intimate muscles clenched around him.

Tight.

That cry she gave . . . it was a cry of relief, born of keen anticipation. As if his rude, gritty touch was what she'd been waiting for all this time.

Touch me. Get me dirty. I don't mind.

"I'll be damned." He blinked away a trickling bead of sweat. "You've been wanting this, too."

She bit her lip and blushed. Her lashes fluttered coyly. "I . . . I don't know what you mean."

Aaron chuckled low, dragging his caress from one breast to the other. Of course she wouldn't admit it so easily. That would spoil the fun for them both.

But he knew the truth now. She'd pictured this. Dreamed of this. Perhaps even sent her hand beneath the coverlet and touched herself while imagining just exactly this.

Damn, he loved her.

And he was going to make this good.

He made his voice low and smug as he thumbed her hardened nipple. Smearing soot in a lewd circle. "Don't play innocent, Miss Highwood. You've been wanting this. A hard, sweaty pounding from the village smith. These strong, dirty hands all over your body. You've been wanting it, haven't you?"

"I . . ."

He withdrew halfway, then slid deep. "Haven't you?"

As he moved in and out, her head bobbed in a subtle nod.

"Say it." He thrust hard.

She gasped. "Yes."

A thrill of triumph buzzed through his whole body—then settled, tense and eager, in the base of his spine.

"Show me, love. Show me how bad you wanted it."

She kissed him deeply, hungrily, catching his tongue and suckling it hard. As they kissed, she made soft, needy whimpers in the back of her throat.

"Take me," she whispered. "Mark me as yours. I want everyone to see."

Her words shredded his restraint, but he fought the urge to pump hard and fast, remaining faithful to the slow, steady grind that made her writhe and moan.

Made her tense and grip tight.

And then at long, merciful last—made her shudder and keen in sweet release.

Thank God.

When she'd recovered from her crisis, he gathered her tight in his arms. Then he stood, lifting her off the anvil entirely and settling her weight against his chest.

"Hold tight," he grunted. "Hold tight to me."

She obeyed, lashing her arms around his neck and legs about his waist.

She wanted a tupping from a coarse, common brute? That's what she'd get. Ten years at this forge had changed him, raised him from a youth to a man. He'd learned patience, attention to detail, restraint—everything he needed to be slow and steady for her pleasure.

But it had also made him strong as an ox. And now it was his turn.

Bracing his feet shoulder-width apart, he tensed his thighs until they were solid as tree trunks. He used every bit of the hard-earned strength in his arms and shoulders, sliding her up and down his length. Using her shamelessly, clutching her bottom with his sooty hands and working her hard.

It wasn't a feat he could have kept up all night, but that didn't matter. His lust had reached such a desperate pitch that a minute or two was all it would take.

If that.

He wanted to keep his eyes open. This was his dream, his fantasy come to life. She was in his arms, all lacy and perfect and dirty and wet. He meant to watch her, keep his gaze on her flushed, glistening cleavage as he came.

But when the pleasure ripped through him, his eyes squeezed shut of their own accord. The fierce jolts of ecstasy sent him someplace dark, and then someplace bright . . .

And then somewhere utterly blank.

Her sweet embrace brought him back. That, and the relentless drumming of the rain.

Somehow he managed to carry her to the table and set her down on the planked surface. He pulled up his trousers and slumped next to her, weak all over.

No more work was getting done on that gate today.

"Oh, Aaron. I'm in such trouble."

Shaking off the postcoital lethargy, he turned and met her gaze. "If you don't . . . I . . ."

"No," she jumped to assure him. "I didn't mean that way. I have no regrets about today. Or last night. None at all."

He exhaled with relief. "Whatever the problem, I'll mend it. That's what I do. I mend things."

"This isn't as simple as a broken latch."

"Whatever it is, whatever it takes, I will mend it. If you don't know it by now . . ." He drew a sooty line down her cheek. "Diana, I love you more than my life."

She bit her lip. "That's just it. *My* life's at stake. I may be charged with a felony."

CHAPTER 12

Diana waited, breathless, for his reaction.

After long, tense moments, he finally gave her one.

He laughed.

She only wished this were a laughing matter. "It's not a joke, I'm afraid. I'm under quite serious suspicion."

"Of what?"

She sat tall on the table, letting her legs dangle over the edge. "When I came down from my chamber this morning, all the ladies were in the dining room. They were whispering about me among themselves. I thought they must have found out about us, about last night. But that wasn't it. Mrs. Nichols accused me of something entirely different. They think I've been stealing."

"Stealing?" He frowned, all amusement gone from his eyes. "You?"

"There's been a rash of small things gone missing from the rooming house."

He nodded. "Charlotte told me about that."

"She did? When?"

He waved off the question. "Not important now. Go on."

As she spoke, she tugged at her soiled bodice, pulling it straight. "Last night, while all the ladies were gone to Ambervale, several more items disappeared. This time, some were valuable. Miss Price is missing a gold brooch, and a guinea was stolen from Mrs. Nichols's own desk. And since I was the only lady who stayed home . . ."

"You couldn't have been the only one there. What about the maids?"

She shook her head. "Only Matilda was there, and she slept in the same room as Mrs. Nichols. If she'd stirred, the landlady would have noticed. In their eyes, I'm the only one who could have taken the things."

"But you didn't."

"Of course I didn't," she said. "I've never stolen in my life. It's clear no one *wants* to believe it was me, but it seems the only logical explanation. They think I've developed a compulsion of some kind. Some sort of illness that drives me to steal."

She exhaled heavily and wove her hands into a tight lattice of interlaced fingers. "Miss Price has requested a magistrate. I have no choice but to tell them the truth. I'll tell them it couldn't have been me, because I was here with you, all night long."

His eyes flared. "What? Diana, you can't tell them that."

The vehemence of his reply took her by surprise. He pushed off the table and went to the forge, raking the coals of the dying fire and feeding it new splits of wood.

"I don't think I have a choice," she said. "It is the truth."

"Yes. And if you tell them, you will be ruined. In truth."

"Better to be a ruined woman than a suspected thief. Don't you agree?"

He didn't agree, nor give any response at all.

"That missing brooch is gold, Aaron. It's worth a great deal. Thieves are hanged for stealing less."

"No one's going to hang *you*. You're not a thief. The items will turn up, or someone else will confess. They have no evidence, only suspicion." He approached her and put his hands on her shoulders. Their weight settled, heavy as a yoke. "Why tell everyone about last night and invite uncharitable gossip?"

She shrugged. "Perhaps I don't care about the gossip."

"I don't believe that."

"Then try a little harder." Diana was frustrated now. Hadn't he promised to trust that she knew her own mind?

She tried to explain. "When I came downstairs this morning and saw them all staring at me, I thought we were found out. For a moment, I was stricken by sheer terror. I was certain I'd be ruined. But then something changed. Once I'd resigned myself to the inevitability . . . I felt strangely free. Unashamed, excited. Aaron, I *want* people to know."

"Well, I don't. Not like this." He released her and began pacing the smithy.

She watched him, perplexed. "I don't understand. Aren't we planning to marry?"

"Aye, but I wanted to wed you in a respectable fashion. If they hear about this, people will think we only married because I seduced you and you had no choice."

"So this is about your pride," she said. "*Your* reputation, not mine."

"It's both, Diana. But yes, I have a reputation, too. People respect me in this village. This is my home."

"I hope it will be my home, as well."

"Then think this through. What if word gets around London that you were defiled by a local craftsman? Good families might stop sending their young ladies to Spindle Cove. The whole village would suffer, and it would be my fault. I might not be able to support you then."

This probably wasn't the time to remind him that her dowry, while modest by aristocratic standards, could keep them comfortable for decades. He would only receive it as another insult.

"Aaron, I don't know what to say. Except that perhaps you should have thought about all this before you carried me to your bed last night."

He rubbed his mouth. "I wasn't thinking last night. Obviously."

Diana struggled to not take offense. She tried, very hard, to interpret his words in the kindest possible light.

When she'd come to his cottage last night, she'd done so with forethought and a full knowledge of the risks. However, he'd been taken by surprise to find her there. *And* he'd been in a vulnerable state, after a long day spent grappling with mortality and fatigue. Perhaps if he'd had time to think it all through, he would have sent her home and not made love to her.

But even so . . . How could he regret it now? What they'd shared had been so wonderful. At least, it had been wonderful for *her*. She felt ready to be with him, marry him, pledge her life to him.

Maybe he didn't feel as ready as she did.

"Aaron, I understand if you're afraid. I'm frightened, too. We knew it wouldn't be easy to announce our plans, even under the best of circumstances. But I don't see a way around telling the truth."

"It's easy," he said. "We wait. In a day or two, this theft business is sure to be resolved. Then I'll propose to you properly."

"What if this theft business isn't resolved? If I'm asked to explain myself, I'm stuck. My choices are between 'suspected thief' and 'known fornicator.' No matter what, I'm never going to be 'Perfect Miss Highwood' again. And it may seem strange, but I'm happy about that. I'm ready to just be me." She looked him in the eye. "So there's the question, I suppose. Do you love *me*? Or just some precious, perfect idea of me?"

His fingers tamed a stray lock of her hair. "Of course I love you. Perfect or not, I think the world of you, Diana. That's why I can't bear for our friends and neighbors to think something less." He swept a gesture down her soiled frock. "I don't want them believing you're this kind of girl."

She flung her arms wide. "Apparently, I *am* this kind of girl. And you didn't seem to mind ten minutes ago."

"That's different. You know it's different. There's what happens between the two of us, and then there's parading it for public view. *We* know how we feel, but to anyone else . . ." He cringed at his dark handprint sprawled lewdly over her breast. "You look like a lightskirt who's entertained a gang of colliers."

She recoiled, stung. "And yet I didn't feel truly dirty until just this moment."

"I didn't mean it that way."

"I know exactly what you mean. You want a lightskirt in your bed at night, and by day you want a perfect virgin." She pressed a hand to her heart. "But I need a man who knows *me*. Who wants *me*. And who isn't afraid or ashamed for the world to see it."

"So now *I'm* ashamed?" His gesture was impatient. "Diana, our night together wouldn't be such a scandal if anyone—your friends, family, neighbors—suspected that you care for me. But they haven't seen the slightest evidence of that. Have they?"

The edge of accusation in his voice cut her deeply. He was right, she supposed. If she had been more forthright about her feelings for Aaron, the truth of last night wouldn't come as such a surprise. For that matter, she wouldn't have needed to lie about a headache in the first place.

"I . . . I'm not a woman who bares her feelings easily." Out of habit, she reached for the vial hanging about her neck. It wasn't there. Her fingers closed on air, and she felt bereft with nothing to cling to. "I've always been reserved."

"Reserved," he echoed. "Until this past week, you barely acknowledged me when we crossed paths in the lane. I've never taken offense. But now you call *me* ashamed? You know that's not fair."

All Diana knew was that she had to leave.

With shaking fingers, she put her clothing to rights as best she could and headed for the door. If he would abandon her to face false accusations of thievery before admitting to his own true actions, there seemed nothing more to discuss. She was on her own.

"Don't go away angry," he said, his tone gentler than before. "We'll reside in this village for the rest of our lives, God willing. In a week, any absurd accusations of theft will be forgotten. But if you tell everyone about last night, the gossip will linger for years. I just want to be careful, that's all."

"I'll be careful. I have a great deal of practice being careful. Don't worry, Aaron." She whirled her cloak about her shoulders and secured it tight in front. "I'll make it home with these stains unseen. No one needs to know about us. Ever."

She slammed the door, and Aaron's ribs rattled with the force of the crash.

Damn. He hadn't handled that well.

With two sisters in his care, Aaron had been on the receiving end of some feminine fury in his life. But Diana's was a first-rate exit. One that begged, *Chase after me. Grovel and plead and promise to give me anything I ask, everything I need.*

He had every intention of doing just that.

Curse it, he never should have made that remark about lightskirts. He'd sounded disgusted by her, when in reality he was only disgusted with himself.

This entire situation was his fault. He never should have allowed her to stay last night. If another man had treated Diana—or any woman, for that matter—this way, Aaron would have raised hell. And the entire village knew it. He was the resident big brother. He *protected* the female contingent of Spindle Cove. But he'd failed to look out for the woman he loved.

He would go to her. Just as soon as he could manage it. First he needed to bathe, change, shave. He'd put on his best coat, gather up a spring flower or two. He supposed he hadn't the time to learn any poetry—but he would bring the ring.

This was their first proper argument, and Aaron didn't dare skimp on the reconciliation. When he did chase after her to fall at her feet and make promises . . . there could be no half measures.

He had to do this with his whole heart—even if it meant risking all.

CHAPTER 13

By the time Diana arrived back in the village center, her hem and slippers were dredged in mud, and the rain had made a proper mop of her hair. With her cloak wrapped tight about her torso, no one could have guessed at the smudges on her frock beneath.

Her swollen eyes and red, sniffling nose could easily be explained away—just products of the damp weather.

She sighed. As always, her delicate health made such a convenient excuse. No one ever had to know if she didn't wish them to.

As it turned out, she didn't need excuses just yet. Other concerns had occupied the Queen's Ruby residents. As the rooming house came into view, Diana saw all the young ladies milling about the front stoop, huddled under the overhang like a clutch of monks in hooded cloaks.

"Oh, there she is." Charlotte ran to Diana's side. "Where have you been?"

"I went for a walk."

"In this?" Her sister tilted her face to the rain, then slid Diana a suspicious look.

"Never mind me. What's going on here?"

"We're just about to go over to the Bull and Blossom, all of us." Charlotte threaded her arm through Diana's. "Miss Price has insisted they clear the place out and search the rooms. She's in a tizzy about that brooch. Says it was an heirloom."

"They're searching the rooms?"

Mama joined them. Billowing along in her massive black cloak, she looked like a vengeful raven.

"This is an outrage," she said bitterly. "After two years of living in this rooming house, we are made to endure such suspicion? I gave them leave to search your chamber, Diana."

"What?"

"There didn't seem any reason not to. You have nothing to hide. Once that horrid Miss Price is satisfied of the fact, we can put all this absurdity behind us." She made a noise of disgust. "And all this for that ugly, outmoded brooch. She ought to thank the soul who relieved her of it."

While Mrs. Nichols and Matilda made a search of the rooming house, all the ladies made the trudge across the village green to the Bull and Blossom, where they settled at every available table. Mama ordered hot tea. Diana wished she dared ask Mr. Fosbury to doctor hers with whiskey. She despised the way all the ladies were staring at her.

She made herself small in her chair and wrapped her cloak tight about her body, praying this would all be over soon.

"Perhaps it's time we left Spindle Cove," she said quietly.

Her mother seized her arm with excitement. "Oh, Diana. If *that* is the happy result of this debacle, then I wish you'd been accused of thievery a year ago. We can go to Town at once. Minerva and Lord Payne will welcome us with open arms."

Diana doubted that "open arms" bit, but she didn't suppose they would be turned away.

"At last you can start moving in the best circles. Where you *belong*. We will make the acquaintance of so many fine gentlemen. Men of wealth and culture and excellent manners."

Diana wanted to weep. She didn't want men of wealth and culture. She wanted Aaron, with his small, homely cottage and his dedication to his craft. Ironically, after all Diana's fears about her mother and society's disapproval, *he* wasn't willing to brave a little gossip for *her*.

"This is ridiculous," Charlotte declared, standing and addressing the unspoken accusation in the room. "The thief wasn't Diana. I know it wasn't." She turned a keen gaze on Miss Bertram, who sat huddled in her cloak in the corner of the room. "*You're* very quiet."

"What do you mean?" Miss Bertram said, shifting evasively. "I was at Ambervale last night, with everyone else. Everyone except Miss Highwood."

The silence fractured into a flurry of whispered suppositions.

Mr. Fosbury, bless him, played peacemaker. He emerged from the kitchen, bearing a tray of teacakes to pass around. "Now, now. I'm sure this is all a misunderstanding. No one who knows Miss Highwood could believe this of her."

Miss Price clucked her tongue. "No one who's lived with her for the past week could deny she's been acting strangely. Disappearing at mealtime, keeping to herself." She confronted Diana directly. "You told everyone you were ill last night. But then you seemed right as roses this morning."

"Yes," Diana said. "Yes, I lied about being ill last night."

This was it. She was going to tell the truth. Even if she had to give up her dreams of being a blacksmith's wife, she refused to surrender her hard-won sense of freedom.

Another of the girls looked perplexed. "Why would you do that, Miss Highwood? Weren't you looking forward to visiting Ambervale?"

"I should think the reason is obvious," Miss Price declared. "She stayed behind so she could make free with our possessions."

"No." Diana pulled her spine straight. "I feigned illness for the same reason I've been feigning ill health for years now. Habit. And fear." She turned to her mother, steeling her resolve. "My asthma hasn't bothered me in years, Mama. I've been told I'm cured. But I've clung to the appearance of delicate health because . . . because it's easier to claim a false malady than endure the real headache of arguing with you."

A hush fell over the room. She could feel everyone staring at her.

"I'm sorry, Mama. I should have been honest and told you I didn't wish to go."

"Why would you not wish to go?" her mother cried. "You had the lead in the theatrical. And I know we agreed on Lord Drewe's unsuitability, but Lord Payne was attending as well. One of them might have invited a highly placed friend."

"I don't care about Lord Drewe," she exclaimed. "Nor his friends. I don't want the same things you want, Mama. Marrying me off to a duke is *your* dream, not mine."

Pursing her mouth in displeasure, Mama flicked open her fan. "I think you *are* ill. I'm sure I've never heard you speak in such a fashion."

"Well, I suggest you get used to it." Diana rose and confronted the room of shocked faces. "I am guilty of falsehood. It was wrong of me to lie. Not only wrong but cowardly as well. I am sorry for it. But I swear to you, I did not steal. They won't find anything in my room."

Matilda came bursting through the door, closely followed by Mrs. Nichols. "We found something in Miss Highwood's room."

"What?" Charlotte cried. "Impossible."

"Is it my brooch?" asked Miss Price.

"Not the brooch," Mrs. Nichols said, giving Diana an apologetic look. "But we did find these."

The old woman unrolled a linen handkerchief to reveal a collection of shiny metallic objects.

Oh, no. They were Aaron's pieces. The ones she'd kept hidden at the bottom of her trousseau.

Diana went dizzy. She sat down again. "I didn't steal those. You can ask Sally Bright."

"Ask me what?" Sally asked, having just popped through the door. She flashed a cheeky smile. "You don't really think I'd miss a scene like this, do you?"

Wonderful. Now the whole village was assembled to witness Diana's humiliation. All the ladies of the Queen's Ruby, Mr. Fosbury and his serving girl, assorted tavern patrons, and now Sally Bright—who would share the tale with the few remaining people in the parish who'd missed it.

"Those pieces Mrs. Nichols is holding. I purchased them from the All Things shop, didn't I?"

"Oh, yes," Sally said, peering at the handful of silver. "Last year, I think. You told me they were going to be Christmas gifts."

"Then why were they buried at the bottom of her trunk?" Matilda asked. "All secret-like."

"It's plain to see what's been going on," Miss Price said. "The pressure of being the perfect daughter has worn on Miss Highwood, and she's developed this compulsion to collect shiny things. At first she bought them, but now she's resorted to stealing. I want to call for a magistrate."

"But she doesn't have your brooch," Charlotte argued.

"Doesn't she? She probably hid it elsewhere." Miss Price ticked off the "evidence" on her fingers. "She lied about being ill. She was the only one with a chance to steal it. She disappeared again this morning, and now we find this cache of trinkets."

"Those are not trinkets," Diana argued. "They're art. They're precious."

"Precious?" Miss Price turned to Mrs. Nichols and raised her eyebrows in a way that said, *See what I mean?*

"I'm sure there's another explanation," Mrs. Nichols said. "Miss Highwood, if you *were* at the rooming house last night, did you hear anyone come in or go out?"

"No," Diana said. "I couldn't have heard."

"Why not?"

"Because I wasn't there."

A ripple of murmurs passed through the tavern.

Mama snorted. "Of course you were there. Charlotte looked in on you when we returned."

"Yes, I know. I was awake. I'd just come back in."

"From where?" Miss Price asked.

Diana buried her face in her hands and rubbed her temples. This was madness. Even if she told the truth, she wasn't sure anyone would believe her. She was about to publicly ruin herself *and* lose Aaron forever.

"She was with me."

Her head and heart lifted at the sound of that familiar baritone.

Aaron.

He stood silhouetted in the door. His hair was damp, plastered to his brow. His boots were caked with mud. He wore the same chocolate-brown coat she'd stitched together minutes after stitching his arm.

And no man had ever looked so handsome.

"She was with me," he repeated, walking into the tavern. "All night long."

Diana wanted to cheer. Charlotte actually *did* cheer, albeit quietly.

"But of course!" Mama exclaimed with evident relief. "This explains everything."

What? Diana hadn't been expecting her mother to take this so well.

She looked around the tavern. *Everyone* seemed to be taking this well.

"Oh, yes," said Mrs. Nichols, catching on to the conclusion that was seemingly obvious to all but Diana. "We all know about Mr. Maidstone's accident yesterday."

Everyone in the tavern nodded and murmured in agreement.

"Mr. Dawes was called away to set a bone. Miss Diana must have heard the news. She was helping nurse an injured man, just like she helped with Finn's surgery."

"That is so like my daughter," Mama crowed. "Always kind to the less fortunate."

Oh, for heaven's sake.

This was ridiculous. Diana couldn't ruin herself when she *tried.*

She caught Aaron's gaze. She knew they were sharing the same thought. They could let the mistaken assumption stand. Everything could be settled without any scandal at all.

But I don't want to hide it, she told him with her eyes.

He nodded in agreement. "It's all right. Tell the truth."

Her heart beat faster. "You're wrong, Mother. I went to Mr. Dawes's cottage *after* he was finished tending to Mr. Maidstone. I . . . I spent the night there."

Her mother laughed, incredulous. "Well, whyever would you do that?"

Diana smacked a palm to her forehead. Did she have to draw every conclusion with pen and ink? "We were making love!"

Now the tavern went stone silent.

Mama snorted. "I'm sure I don't believe *that.* I'd sooner believe you were a thief."

"It's the truth, Mrs. Highwood," Aaron said. "Whether you believe it or not. And I'm here to ask Miss Highwood to marry me."

From his breast pocket he removed a ring and laid it on

the table. A gold band shaped like two entwined vines, with golden leaves bracketing a ruby-and-diamond bloom.

She pressed a hand to her heart. Oh, it was lovely. His best work yet. How he must have slaved over the design.

"Miss Highwood." Aaron cleared his throat and moved as though he would kneel. "Diana, I—"

"Stop!" Mama cried.

Aaron froze in an awkward half crouch.

"How can you expect me to allow this?" Mama glared at him. "How dare you impugn my Diana's honor in this fashion! Grasping, awful man. Of course you'd leap at the opportunity to rescue her from these silly thieving suspicions, hoping she'll marry you in gratitude. It's not as though a man like you would have a chance at her otherwise. But I tell you, your scheme won't work."

"It's not a scheme," Diana said. "And he has more than 'a chance' with me, Mama. I love Aaron. And I am going to marry him."

Diana reached for the ring he'd laid on the table.

Her mother smacked her hand away. *Smacked* it, as though Diana were a three-year-old child.

Diana simmered with anger. She was not a child. She was all grown up, and her mother was about to learn the truth of it.

"Mama," she said coolly, "listen to me closely. I am in love with Mr. Dawes. I have been for some time. I collected his pieces from the All Things shop because I admired him. We shared our first kiss in the vicar's curricle. He introduced me to his sister on our excursion to Hastings. I tried to kill an eel for him. I shot at a robber who threatened him. And last night . . . ?" She lifted her voice. "We. Were. Making. Love. In a bed. All night long. It was hot and sweaty and glorious. I left scratches on his back. He has a freckle just to the right of his navel. And if you don't believe all that . . ."

She ripped her cloak open and threw it aside, exposing Aaron's black, sooty handprint on her breast. "Here. See for yourself."

Several moments passed, during which the only sound was the mad thump of her heartbeat in her ears.

Then someone shrieked.

Strange. Diana had expected a measure of shock at her revelations, but that seemed a bit extreme, *shrieking*.

Now another girl screamed.

And another. "It's a rat!"

A rat?

Oh, God. It *was* a rat. A long-tailed, bewhiskered rat, big as a bread loaf, with a pink, twitching nose. The creature scampered onto the table—and absconded with the ring.

Her ring.

Aaron cursed and lunged to get it back.

"Mr. Evermoore!" Miss Bertram leaped to her feet. "Mr. Evermoore, no! You come back here right now."

In an instant, the tavern was in upheaval. Some of the ladies jumped on chairs and tables. Others reached for any makeshift truncheon close at hand. Pots, pans, stray copies of *Mrs. Worthington's Wisdom.*

"I knew it!" Charlotte cried in vindication. "I knew all along the thief had to be Miss Bertram."

"I don't think it was her," Diana said. "I mean, obviously

it was her . . . her pet. She must have left the rat behind last night while everyone went to Ambervale."

"The little bastard's over here," Mr. Fosbury shouted. "In the kitchen."

There was a crash of glass. Followed by an explosion of flour.

Mama crumpled into the nearest chair, her eyes rolling back in a dead faint. Just as well.

"Oh, please don't kill him!" Miss Bertram sobbed. "He can't help taking things. But he's so intelligent. You don't understand. Oh, Mr. Evermoore."

Diana cringed at her sister. " 'No one understands our attachment.' Isn't that what she always said?"

Charlotte shuddered. "I don't understand it, either. I don't want to."

The two of them laughed uneasily.

Of all the potential scandals that could have lessened Diana's sordid revelation . . . this one would serve. Yes, she'd given her heart and her virtue to the local blacksmith. At least she wasn't in love with a rat.

"Found it." Aaron's dark head popped up from the other side of the bar. He called to her. "I found the ring."

Diana pushed through the crowd to meet him at the bar. But she couldn't bear to remain separated from him, so she scrambled atop the counter on hands and knees.

He did the same.

They sat together, cross-legged atop the lacquered surface, while the wild rat hunt proceeded all around them.

Aaron huffed his breath, blowing a bit of flour off the jeweled setting. He shined the band with his sleeve. "I'd make a speech, but—"

She laughed and flicked a glance at the ongoing melee. "Just put it on, and quick."

She offered her hand. He slid the ring on her finger.

"Oh, Aaron." Emotion frayed her voice. "It's beautiful."

"Not as beautiful as you."

He cupped her cheek in one of his strong workman's hands and tilted her face to his.

And when he kissed her, the world went away.

"Wh- . . . Oh, where am I? Oh, my nerves."

Diana winced, suddenly conscious of their surroundings. Her mother had revived just in time to see them embracing atop the bar counter, coated in flour and mud and soot, and locked in a deep, passionate kiss.

"Wonderful news, Mama." Diana held up her left hand and waggled her ring finger. "I'm finally engaged."

Her mother blinked at the ring. Blinked at Aaron.

And promptly fainted once again.

A few weeks later

"Are you very sure, my dear? It's not too late to change your mind."

Diana shook her head.

From the vestibule, she stood on tiptoe and peered down the long aisle of St. Ursula's, festooned with bunting and posies of daffodils. All their family, friends, and neighbors sat crowding the pews in anticipation.

"Mama, the wedding will begin any moment. And it can't start soon enough for me. I'm not going to change my mind."

"I had to ask." Her mother twisted a lace handkerchief in her hand. "I know you girls think me a silly, overwrought creature who thinks of nothing but marrying you to rich gentlemen. But it's only because I love you so."

Diana softened. "I know, Mama."

"After we lost your father, I was anxious every moment. How would we live? Where would we go? How could I provide the best for you?" She dabbed at her eyes. "I only wanted to spare you girls the same nervousness."

Diana's heart twisted in her chest. "I understand. I do, and I love you for it. Please be happy for me today. I promise, you will never need to worry for me again. With Aaron, I will be loved and safe and protected. Always."

"I suppose that is all I can ask." Mama noisily blew her nose into the handkerchief. "Oh, but I had such dreams for you. My intuition insisted that one day a handsome duke would roll into this village in a splendid carriage, ready to choose his bride. But I suppose it's not likely to happen."

"I suppose not," Diana said. "And even if it did, I would still marry Aaron."

Mama grasped her hand and squeezed it fondly. "Mr. Dawes may not be a gentleman, but your ring *is* nicer than Minerva's. There is that."

Diana smiled. Some things never changed.

"Are we ready?" Colin Sandhurst, Lord Payne, appeared in the vestibule, looking as handsomely attired as always and quite ready to have this done.

He offered an arm to Mama and walked her down the aisle. Charlotte followed, fizzing with joy for her role as bridesmaid—or at least, for the new frock it occasioned.

Diana brought up the end of the procession.

As she walked down the grand, carpeted aisle, moving ever closer to the handsome, broad-shouldered figure at the front of the church, she saw their whole future painted for them in rich, stained-glass hues. They would marry here. They would make Christmas and Easter memories here. They would christen their children here.

If her arithmetic was correct, they could be doing that christening part in a little less than nine months. She hadn't given Aaron any idea—it was too early yet to be sure. But she thought he might have formed his own suspicions.

As the organist played the last verse of the hymn, he drifted close. His strong arm brushed hers, and a shiver of delight passed through her. Strangely enough, she couldn't gather the courage to look up at his face. Her whole heart would be in her eyes, she knew. And though her heart would be forever his by the end of this ceremony, she wanted to guard it just a few moments more.

"You are radiant," he murmured. "And you look like a woman with a secret."

"Just a little wedding present for you," she whispered. "You'll find out later."

"Good. Because I have a present for us both."

"Oh?"

He leaned and spoke in her ear. "I hired a cook."

She had to clap her hand over her mouth to keep from laughing aloud. Oh, she loved him so.

"Who gives this woman to be married to this man?" The vicar looked to Lord Payne, who was standing in the first row.

Luckily, her brother-in-law remained enough of a scoundrel to be easily corrupted. As she'd asked of him, he remained silent.

"I do." Diana looked up at Aaron and smiled. "I give myself."

Not ready to leave Spindle Cove yet?
Keep reading for an exclusive, extra-long peek
at Tessa Dare's delightful

ANY DUCHESS WILL DO

Coming soon from Avon Books

CHAPTER ONE

Griff cracked open a single eyelid. A bright stab of pain told him he'd made a grave mistake. He quickly shut his eye again and put a hand over it, groaning.

Something had gone horribly wrong.

He needed a shave. He needed a bath. He might need to be sick. Attempts to summon any recollection of the previous evening resulted in another sharp slice of agony.

He tried to ignore the throb in his temples and focused on the tufted, plush surface under his back. It wasn't his bed. Perhaps not even a bed at all. Was it just a trick of his nausea, or was the damned thing moving?

"Griff." The voice came to him through a thick, murky haze. It was muffled, but unmistakably female.

God's knees, Halford. The next time you decide to bed a woman after a months-long drought, at least stay sober enough to remember it afterward.

He cursed his stupidity. The epic duration of his celibacy was no doubt the reason he'd been tempted by . . . whoever she was. He had no idea of her name or her face. Just a vague impression of a feminine presence nearby. He inhaled and smelled perfume of an indeterminate, expensive sort.

Damn. He'd need jewels to get out of this, no doubt.

Something dull and pointed jabbed his side. "Wake up."

Did he know that voice? Keeping one hand clapped over his eyes, he fumbled about with the other hand. He caught a handful of heavy silk skirt and skimmed his touch downward until his fingers closed around a stocking-clad ankle. Sighing a little in apology, he rubbed his thumb up and down.

A squawk of feminine outrage assailed his ears. An unyielding object cracked him over the head, but hard. Now to the pounding and throbbing in his skull, he could add ringing.

"Griffin Eliot York. Really."

Bloody hell.

Forget the headache and piercing sunlight, he bolted upright—bashing his head again, this time on the low ceiling. Blinking, he confirmed the unthinkable truth. He wasn't in his bedchamber—or any bedchamber—but in the coach. And the woman seated across from him was all too familiar, with the double strand of rubies at her throat and her elegant sweep of silver hair.

They stared at one another in mutual horror.

"Mother?"

She smacked him again with her collapsed parasol. "Wake up."

"I'm awake, I'm awake." When she readied another blow, he held up his hands in surrender. "Good God. I may never sleep again."

Though the air in the coach was oven-warm, he shuddered. Now he most definitely needed a bath.

He peered out the window and saw nothing but vast expanses of rolling green, dappled with cloud-shaped shadows. The coach's truncated shadow indicated midday.

"Where the devil are we? And why?"

He tried to piece together memories of the previous evening. This was hardly the first time he'd woken in unfamiliar surroundings, head ringing and stomach achurn . . . but it was the first time in a good long while. He thought he'd put this sort of debauchery behind him. So what had happened?

He hadn't imbibed more than his usual amount of wine at dinner. By the fish course, however, he seemed to recall the china's acanthus pattern undulating. Swimming before his eyes.

After that, he recalled . . . nothing.

Damn. He'd been drugged.

Kidnapped.

He snapped to alert, bracing his boots on the carriage floorboards.

Whoever his captors were, he must assume they were armed. He was without a blade, without a gun—but he had eager fists, honed reflexes, and a rapidly clearing head. On his own, he would have given himself even chances. But the bastards had taken his mother, too.

"Do not be alarmed," he told her.

"Oh, I wouldn't dream of it. Bad for the complexion." She touched the double strand of rubies at her throat.

Those rubies. They gave him pause.

What shoddy excuse for a kidnapper used the family coach and left the captive wearing several thousand pounds' worth of jewels?

Devil take it.

"*You.*"

"Hm?" His mother raised her eyebrows, all innocence.

"You did this. You put something in my wine at dinner and stuffed me in the carriage." He pushed a hand through his hair. "My God. I can't believe you."

She looked out the window and shrugged. Or rather, she gave the duchess version of a shrug—a motion that didn't involve anything so common or gauche as the flexing of shoulder muscles, but merely a subtle tilt of the head. "You'd never have come if I *asked.*"

Incredible.

Griff closed his eyes. Times like these, he supposed he ought to remind himself that a man only had one mother, and his mother only had one son, and she'd carried him in her womb and toiled in labor and so on and so forth. But he did not wish to think about her womb right now—not when he was still trying, desperately, to forget that she possessed ankles.

"Where are we?" he asked.

"Sussex."

Sussex. One of the few counties in England where he didn't claim any property. "And what is the purpose of this urgent errand?"

A faint smile curved her lips. "We're going to meet your future bride."

He stared at his mother. Many moments passed before he could manage coherent speech.

"You are a scheming, fiendish woman with entirely too much time at leisure."

"And you are the eighth Duke of Halford," she returned. "I know that doesn't mean much to you. The disgraces at Oxford, the gambling, the years of aimless debauchery . . . You seem determined to be nothing more than an unfortunate blot on the distinguished Halford legacy. At the very least, start on the next generation while I still have time to mold it. You have a responsibility to—"

"To continue the line." He closed his eyes and pinched the bridge of his nose. "So I've been told. Again and again."

"You'll be five-and-thirty this year, Griffy."

"Yes. Which makes me much too old to be called 'Griffy.'"

"More to the point, I am fifty-eight. I need grandchildren before my decline. It's not right for two generations of the family to be drooling at the same time."

"Your decline?" He laughed. "Tell me, Mother, how can I hasten that happy process? Other than offering a firm push."

Her eyebrow arched in amusement. "Just try it."

Griff sighed. His mother was . . . his mother. There was no other woman in England like her, and the rest of the world had better pray God had broken the mold. Like the jewels she delighted in wearing, Judith York was a formidable blend of exterior polish and inner fire.

For most of the year, they led entirely separate lives. They only resided in the same house for these few months of the London season. Apparently, even that was too much.

"I've been patient," she said. "Now I'm desperate. You must marry, and it must be soon. I've tried to find the most accomplished young beauties in England to tempt you. And I did, but you ignored them. I finally realized the answer is not quality. It's quantity."

"*Quantity?* Are you taking me to some free-love utopian commune where men are permitted as many wives as they please?"

"Don't be ridiculous."

"I was being hopeful."

Her lip curled in a delicate scowl. "You're terrible."

"Thank you. I work hard at it."

"So I've often lamented. If only you applied the same effort toward . . . anything else."

Griff closed his eyes. If there was any conversation more tired and repetitive than the "When will you ever marry?" debate, it was the "You're a grave disappointment" harangue. Only in *this* family would it be considered "disappointing" to successfully oversee a vast fortune, six estates, several hundred employees, and thousands of tenants. Impressive, by most standards. But in the Halford line? Not quite enough. Unless a man was reforming Parliament or discovering a new trade route to Patagonia, he just didn't measure up.

He glanced out the window again. They seemed to be entering a sort of village. He slid open the glass pane and discovered he could smell the sea. A salted-blue freshness mingled with the greener scents of countryside.

"It is a prettyish sort of place," his mother said. "Very tidy and quiet. I can understand why it's so popular with the young ladies."

The coach rolled to a halt in the center of the village, near a wide, pleasant green that ringed a grand medieval church. He peered out the window, gazing in all directions. The place was far too small to be Brighton or . . .

"Wait a minute." A vile suspicion formed in his mind.

Surely she hadn't . . .

She *wouldn't.*

The liveried footman opened the coach door. "Good day, your graces. We've reached Spindle Cove."

"**O**h, *bollocks.*"

When the fancy coach came trundling down the lane, Pauline scarcely gave it a glance. Many a fine carriage had come down that same road, bringing one visitor or another to the village. A holiday in Spindle Cove was said to cure any gently bred lady's crisis of confidence.

But Pauline wasn't a gently bred lady, and her trials were more practical in nature. Such as the fact that she'd just stumbled into a murky puddle, splashing her hem with mud.

And that her sister was near tears for the second time that morning.

"The list," Daniela said. "It's not here."

Drat. Pauline knew they didn't have time to go back to the farm. She was due at the tavern in minutes. This was Saturday—the day of the Spindle Cove ladies' weekly salon, and the Bull and Blossom's busiest day of the week. Mr. Fosbury was a fair-minded employer, but he docked wages for tardiness. And Father noticed.

Frantic, Daniela fished in her pocket. Her eyes welled with tears. "It's not here. It's not here."

"Never mind. I remember it." Shaking the muddy droplets from her skirts, Pauline ticked the items off in her memory. "Dried currants, worsted thread, a bit of sponge. Oh, and powdered alum. Mother needs it for pickling."

When they entered the Brights' All Things shop, they found it packed to bursting. While the visiting ladies met for their weekly salon, the villagers purchased their dry goods. Villagers like Mrs. Whittlecombe, a cobwebby old widow who only left her decrepit farmhouse once a week to stock up on comfits and "medicinal" wine. The woman gave them a disdainful sniff as Pauline and Daniela wedged their way into the shop.

Pauline could just make out two flashes of white-blond hair on the other side of the counter. Sally Bright was busy with customers three deep, and her younger brother Rufus ran back and forth from the storeroom.

Fortunately, the Simms sisters had been friends with the Bright family since as far back as any of them could remember. They needn't wait to be helped.

"Put the eggs away," Pauline told her sister. "I'll fetch the sponge and thread from the storeroom. You get the currants and alum. Two measures of currants, one of alum."

Daniela carefully set the basket of brown speckled eggs on the counter and went to a row of bins. Her lips moved as she scanned for the one labeled CURRANTS. Then she frowned with concentration as she sifted the contents into a rolled cone of brown paper.

Once she'd seen her sister settle to the task, Pauline gathered the needed items from the back. When she returned, Daniela was waiting with goods in hand.

"Too much alum," Pauline said, inspecting. "It was meant to be just one measure."

"Oh. Oh, no."

"It's all right," she said in a calm voice. "Easily mended. Just put the extra back."

She hoped her sister didn't notice the sneering expression on old Mrs. Whittlecombe's face.

"I don't know that I can continue to give this shop my custom," the old woman said. "Allowing half-wits behind the counter."

Sally Bright gave the woman a flippant smile. "Just tell me when we can stop stocking your laudanum, Mrs. Whittlecombe."

"That's a health tonic."

"Of course it is," Sally said dryly.

Pauline went to the ledger to record their purchases. She secretly loved this part. She flipped through the pages slowly, taking her time to peruse Sally's notes and tabulations.

Someday she'd have her own shop, keep her own ledgers. It was a dream she hadn't shared with anyone—not even her closest friend. Just a promise she recited to herself, when the hours of farm and serving work lay heavy on her shoulders.

Someday.

She found the correct page. After the credit they earned from bringing in eggs, they only owed sixpence for the rest of their shopping. Good.

Bang.

She whipped her head up, startled.

"Good gracious, child! What on earth are you doing?" Mrs. Whittlecombe slapped the counter again.

"I . . . I'm p-puttin' back the alum," Daniela stammered.

"That's not 'da aw-wum,'" the old woman repeated, mocking Daniela's thick speech. "That's the sugar."

Oh, bollocks. Pauline winced. She knew she should have done it herself. But she'd wanted so fiercely for Daniela to show that wretched old bat she could do it.

Now the wretched old bat cackled in triumph.

Confused, Daniela smiled and tried to laugh along.

Pauline's heart broke for her sister. They were only a year apart in age, but so many more in understanding. Of all the things that came a bit more difficult for Daniela than other people—pronouncing words that ended in consonants, subtracting from numbers greater than ten—cruelty seemed the hardest concept for her to grasp. A mercy, in Amos Simms's family.

"Not the clayed sugar," Rufus Bright moaned.

Sally boxed him across the ear.

"I just scraped it from the cone," he apologized, rubbing the side of his head. "Bin was almost full."

"Well, it's entirely useless now," said Mrs. Whittlecombe smugly.

"I'll pay for the sugar," Pauline said. She felt instantly nauseous, as if she'd swallowed five pounds of the stuff raw. Fine white sugar came dear.

"You don't have to do that," Sally said in a low voice. "We're practically sisters. We should be *real* sisters, if my brother Errol had any sense in his head."

Pauline shook her head. She'd ceased pining for Errol Bright when they parted ways years ago. She certainly didn't want to be indebted to him now.

"I'll pay for it," she insisted. "It was my mistake. I should have done it myself, but I was in a hurry."

And now she would certainly be late for her post at the Bull and Blossom. This day only grew worse and worse.

Sally looked pained, caught between the need to turn a profit and the desire to help a friend.

In the corner, Daniela had finally realized the consequences of her error. "I can put it back," she said, scooping from the sugar barrel and dumping it into the alum, muddling both quantities with her flowing tears. "I can put it right."

"It's all right, dear." Pauline went to her side and gently removed the tin scoop from her sister's hand. "Go on," she told Sally firmly. "I think I have some credit in the ledger."

She didn't just *think* she had credit. She *knew* she did. Several pages beyond the Simms family account, there was a page labeled simply PAULINE—and it showed precisely two pounds, four shillings, and eight pence of credit accrued. For the past few years, she'd saved and scrimped every penny she could, trusting Sally's ledger with the safekeeping. It was the closest thing to a bank account a serving girl like her could have.

Almost a year, she'd been saving. Saving for something better, for her and Daniela both. Saving for *someday*.

"Do it," she said.

With a few strokes of Sally's quill, the money was almost entirely gone. Eleven shillings, eight pence left.

"I didn't charge for the alum," Sally murmured.

"Thank you." Small comfort, but it was something. "Rufus, would you kindly walk my sister home? I'm due at the tavern, and she's upset."

Rufus, apparently ashamed of his earlier behavior, offered his arm. "'Course I will. Come along, Danny. I'll drive you in the cart."

When Daniela resisted, Pauline hugged her and whispered, "You go home, and tonight I'll bring your penny."

The promise brightened Daniela's face. It was her daily

task to gather the eggs, count and candle them, and prepare them to sell. In return, Pauline gave her a penny a week.

Every Saturday evening she watched Daniela carefully add the coin to an old, battered tea tin. She would shake the tin and grin, satisfied with the rattling sound. It was a ritual that pleased them both. The next morning the same treasured penny went into the church offering—every Sunday, without fail.

"Go on, then." She sent her sister off with a smile she didn't quite feel.

Once Rufus and Daniela had left, Mrs. Whittlecombe crowed with satisfaction. "That'll be a lesson for you, bringing a simpleton around the village."

"Go easy, Mrs. Whittlecombe," a bystander said. "You know they mean well."

Pauline flinched inwardly. Not that phrase. She'd heard it countless times over the course of her life. Always in that same pitying tone, usually accompanied by a clucking tongue: *Can't be hard on those Simms girls . . . you know they mean well.*

In other words, no one expected them to *do* a cursed thing right. How could they? Two unwanted daughters in a family with no sons. One simple-minded, the other lacking in every feminine grace.

Just once, Pauline wanted to be known not for *meaning* well, but for *doing* well.

That day wouldn't be today. Not only had everything gone wrong, but as she regarded Mrs. Whittlecombe, Pauline couldn't muster any good intentions. Anger bloomed in her chest like a predatory vine, all sharp needles and grasping tendrils.

The old woman placed two bottles of tonic in her netted bag. They clinked together in a way that only increased Pauline's anger. "Next time, keep the fool thing at home."

Her hands balled into tight fists at her side. Of course she wouldn't lash out at an old woman the way she'd once fought the teasing boys at school, but the motion was instinctive. "Daniela is not a thing. She is a person."

"She's a half-wit. She doesn't belong out of the house."

"She made a mistake. Just like all people make mistakes." Pauline reached for the bin of ruined white sugar. It was hers now, wasn't it? She'd paid for the contents. "For example, everyone knows I'm incurably clumsy."

"Pauline," Sally warned. "Please don't."

Too late. With an angry heave, she launched the bin's contents into the air.

The room exploded in a blizzard of white, and Mrs. Whittlecombe was at the storm's dead center, sputtering and cursing through a cloud of powder. When the flurries cleared, she looked like Lot's wife, only turned to a pillar of sugar rather than salt.

The sense of divine retribution that settled on Pauline . . . it was almost worth all that hard-earned money.

Almost.

She tossed the empty bin to the floor. "Oh, dear. How stupid of me."

Griff regarded his mother and that smug smile curving her lips. This time she'd gone too far. This wasn't mere meddling. It was diabolical.

Not *Spinster* Cove.

He'd never visited the place, but he knew it well by reputation. This seaside hamlet was where old maids went to embroider and consumptives went to dry.

Accepting the footman's hand, the duchess alighted from the coach. "I understand this place is just bursting with well-bred, unmarried young ladies."

She motioned toward a lodging house. A sign dangling above the entrance announced it as THE QUEEN'S RUBY.

Griff blinked at the green shutters and cheery window boxes stuffed with geraniums. He'd rather bathe in water teeming with sharks.

He turned and walked in the opposite direction.

"Where are you going?" she asked, following.

"There." He nodded at a tavern across the square. By squinting at the sign hung over the red-painted door, he discerned it was called the Bull and Blossom. "I'm going to have a pint of ale and something to eat."

"What about me?"

He gestured expansively. "Make yourself comfortable. Take a suite at the rooming house. Enjoy the healthful sea breezes. I'll send the coach for you in a few weeks." He added under his breath, "Or years."

The footman followed a respectful pace behind, holding the open parasol to shade the duchess.

"Absolutely not," she said. "You're going to select a bride, and you're going to do it today."

"Don't you understand what sort of young ladies are sent to this village? The unmarriageable ones."

"Exactly. It's perfect. None of them will turn you down."

Her words drew Griff to a sharp halt. He swiveled to face her. "Turn *me* down?"

For the obvious reasons, he avoided discussing his *affaires* with her. But the reason he'd been celibate lo these many months had nothing to do with women turning him down. There were many women—beautiful, sophisticated, sensual women—who'd gladly welcome him to their beds this very evening. He was tempted to tell her so, but a man couldn't say such things to his own mother.

She seemed to interpret his silence easily enough.

"I'm not speaking of carnality. I'm speaking of your desirability as a husband. Your reputation leaves a great deal to be desired." She brushed some dust from his sleeve. "Then there's the aging problem."

"The 'aging' problem?" He was thirty-four. By his estimation, his cock had a good three decades of working order ahead, at least.

"To be sure, you're good-looking enough. But there are handsomer."

"Are you sure you're my mother?"

She turned and walked on. "The fact is, most ladies of the *ton* have given you up as a marriage prospect. A village of desperate spinsters is precisely what we need. You must admit, this worked nicely for that scampish friend of yours, Lord Payne."

God's knees. So *that's* what was behind this. Curse that rogue Colin Sandhurst and his bespectacled, bookish bride. Last year, his old gambling friend had been sequestered in this seaside village without funds, and he'd broken free by eloping with a bluestocking. The pair had even stopped at

Winterset Grange, Griff's country retreat, on their way to Scotland.

But their situations were completely different. Griff wasn't desperate for funds in any way. Neither was he desperate for companionship.

Marriage simply wasn't in the cards for him.

His mother fixed him with a look. "Were you waiting to fall in love?"

"What?"

"It's a simple question. Have you delayed marriage all these years because you're waiting to fall in love?"

A simple question, she called it. The answers were anything but.

He could have taken her into the tavern, ordered a few large glasses of wine, and taken an hour or two to explain everything. That he wouldn't be marrying this season, or any season. Her only son would not be merely a blot on the distinguished Halford line, but the very end of it, forever, and the family legacy she held so dear was destined for obscurity. Her hopes of grandchildren would come to naught.

But he couldn't bring himself to do it. Not even today, when she was at her most infuriating. Better to remain a dissolute-yet-redeemable rascal in her eyes than be the son who calmly, irrevocably, broke his mother's heart.

"No," he told her honestly. "I'm not waiting to fall in love."

"Well, that's convenient. We can settle this in one morning. Never mind finding the most polished young beauty in England. You choose a girl—any girl—and I'll polish her myself. Who could better prepare the future Duchess of Halford than the current Duchess of Halford?"

They'd reached the tavern entrance. His mother stared pointedly at the door latch. The footman jumped to open it.

"Oh, look," she said upon entering. "What luck. Here they are."

Griff looked. The scene was even ghastlier than he could have imagined.

This tavern didn't seem to be a "tavern" at all, but more of a tea shop. Young ladies crowded the establishment, all of them hunched over tables and frowning in concentration. They appeared to be engaged in one of those absurd handicrafts that passed for female "accomplishment" these days. Quilling paper, it looked like. They weren't even using fresh parchment—just ripping pages straight from books to fashion their queer little trivets and tea trays.

He peered at the nearest stack of volumes. *Mrs. Worthington's Wisdom for Young Ladies*, each one read. Appalling.

This was everything he'd been avoiding for years. A roomful of unmarried, uninspiring young women, from which the common wisdom would argue he should find a suitable bride.

At the nudging of a friend, one young woman rose from her chair and curtsied. "May we help you, ma'am?"

"Your grace."

The young woman's brow creased. "Ma'am?"

"I am the Duchess of Halford. You would properly address me as 'your grace.'"

"Ah. I see." As her nudging friend smothered a nervous giggle, the fair-haired young woman began again. "May we help you, your grace?"

"Just stand tall, girl. So my son can see you." She turned

her head, surveying the rest of the room. "All of you, on your feet. Best posture."

Pain forked through Griff's skull as chair legs screeched against floorboards. One by one the young ladies obediently rose to their feet.

He noted a few pockmarks. One case of crooked teeth. They were none of them hideous, just—fragile in some cases. Others were unfashionably browned from the sun.

"Well," the duchess said, striding into the center of the room. "Jewels in the rough. In some cases, very rough. But they are all from good family, so with a bit of polish . . ." She turned to him. "Take your choice, Halford. Select any girl who strikes your fancy. I will make her into a duchess."

Every jaw in the room dropped.

Every jaw, that was, except Griff's.

He massaged his throbbing temples and began preparing a little speech in his mind. *Ladies, I beg you. Pay this raving madwoman no attention. She's entered her decline.*

But then, he thought—a quick exit was too kind to her. Surely the only proper punishment was the opposite: to do precisely as his mother asked.

He said, "You claim you can make any one of these girls into a suitable duchess."

"Of course I can."

"And who will be the judge of your success?"

She lifted a brow. "Society, of course. Choose your young lady, and she'll be the toast of London by season's end."

"The toast of London, you say?" He gave a doubtful laugh.

He scanned the tavern for a second time, planning to declare mad, instantaneous love for the most shrinking, awkward, homely chit available—and then watch his mother sputter and flail in response.

However, from the amused glances the young ladies exchanged, Griff could sense that there was more courage and wit in the room than his first impression might have indicated. These young women were no fools. And though they each had their flaws and imperfections—who didn't?—none were unsuitable to a shocking, insurmountable degree.

Damn. He'd looked forward to teaching his overstepping mother a lesson. As matters stood, he supposed he'd be better served to just mutter a few apologies, drag the duchess back to the carriage, and drop her at Bedlam on the way home.

And then, with a creak of hinges and a slam of the rear door—

His salvation arrived.

She came stumbling through the back entrance of the tavern, red-faced and breathless. Her boots and hem were spattered with alarming amounts of mud, and a strange white powder clung to her everywhere else.

A serving girl's apron hung loose around her neck. As she gathered the tapes and knotted them behind her back, the cinch of laces revealed a slender, almost boyish figure. Less of a shapely hourglass, more of a sturdy hitching post.

"It's ten past, Pauline." The male voice boomed from the kitchen.

She called back, "Beggin' pardon, Mr. Fosbury. I'll not be tardy again."

Her diction and accent were not merely uneducated and

rural—they were odd. When she turned, Griff could make out the reason why. She had a hairpin clenched in her teeth like a cheroot, and she mumbled her words around it.

The tardy serving girl clutched another hairpin in her hand, and when her eyes—leaf-green, bright with intelligence—met Griff's, she froze in the act of jamming that pin through the tangle of hair piled atop her head.

God, that hair. He'd heard ladies describe their coiffures as "knots" or "buns." This could only be called a "nest." He was certain he glimpsed a few blades of straw and grass in there.

Clearly, she'd been hoping to enter unnoticed. Instead, she was suddenly the center of attention. That mysterious white powder that clung to her . . . it caught the light, shooting off tiny sparks.

He couldn't look away.

As the breathless young woman alternated glances between Griff, his mother, and the amused ladies filling the rest of the room, her unfinished coiffure disintegrated. Locks of unpinned hair tumbled to her shoulders, surrendering to gravity or indignity, or both.

This would be where the average serving girl would duck her head, flee the room, and await her employer's wrath. No doubt there'd be sniffling or sobbing involved.

But not this serving girl, apparently. This one had just enough pride to trump etiquette *and* good sense.

With a defiant toss of her head to distribute her brandy-colored locks, she turned and spat the last hairpin aside.

"Bollocks," he heard her mutter.

Suddenly, Griff found himself battling a grin. She was perfect. Coarse, uneducated, utterly graceless. A touch too pretty. A plainer girl would have better suited his purpose. But fair looks notwithstanding, she'd do.

"Her," he said. "I'll take her."

CHAPTER TWO

Another girl's prince has arrived.

That was Pauline's first thought, when she stumbled in and spied the finely dressed man silhouetted in the door.

She watched it happen every few months in this village. These young ladies sought refuge in Spindle Cove for the oddest of reasons. Their harp-playing lacked grace, perhaps, or the color of their eyes was unfashionable at Court this season. And then—to the utter astonishment of everyone except Pauline—some handsome earl or viscount or officer came along and married them.

None of them spared so much as a glance for the serving girl.

So which lady was this one after? Whoever she was, she'd be set for life. Everything about the man's appearance—from ivory buttons to fitted leather gloves—blared his wealth in trumpet notes. And if his garments screamed "riches," everything beneath them spoke of power. It would be easy for a gentleman to go soft and paunchy, but he hadn't. The close cut of his dark green topcoat revealed broad shoulders and defined muscles in his upper arms.

His face was strong, too. Boldly sloped nose, squared jaw, and a wide, confident mouth. There was nothing pretty about his features, but when taken together, they had an undeniable masculine appeal.

In short, he was no trial to look at. But even if he weren't—Pauline couldn't take her eyes off the man.

Because he wasn't taking his eyes off her.

And the way he looked at her—like she was the answer to every question he'd never thought to ask—had her heart beating faster than a trapped hare's.

"Her," he said. "I'll take her."

"You can't choose her," an older woman replied, clearly testy. "That's the serving girl."

Pauline spared the lady a brief glance, sizing her up as a silver-haired woman who was small of stature and long on self-importance. She had a rail-straight spine. She'd need it, to hold up that unholy ransom in jewels.

"She's a girl," the man replied evenly, still looking at Pauline. "She's a girl, and she's in the room. You said I might choose any girl in the room."

"She wasn't in the room when I said that."

"She's in the room now. And once I saw her, I had eyes for no one else. She's perfect."

Perfect?

Pauline looked to the window, expecting a pig to fly through it. A pig strumming a lyre and speaking Welsh, perhaps.

The gentleman moved toward her, navigating the room with ease. As he approached, each heavy, rhythmic footfall made her acutely aware of her wild, sugar-dusted hair and mud-spattered hem. She took comfort from the signs of his own flawed humanity. On closer view, he was unshaven, and his eyes were rimmed with red—from lack of sleep or too much drink, or both.

Pauline inhaled slowly. His clothing carried the fading whiff of some masculine, musky cologne. The scent curled inside her, warming her in low, secret places.

"Tell me your name," he said.

He spoke in a voice that was low and rich and . . . magnetic, apparently. She could feel every person in the room sway in his direction, to better make out his words.

"I'm Pauline, sir. Pauline Simms."

"Your age."

"Twenty-three."

"And are you married or betrothed?"

She bit back a startled laugh. "No, sir. I'm not."

"Excellent." He inclined his head. "I am Griffin Eliot York, the eighth Duke of Halford."

A duke?

"Oh, Lord," she muttered.

"Actually, Simms, what you're meant to say is, 'your grace.'"

She dropped her gaze to the floorboards and made an off-balance curtsy. "Your grace."

Waving off her belated attempts at deference, he went on. "My mother has grown impatient with my unmarried state. She enjoined me to take my choice of any woman in this room, with the promise that she could make that woman into a duchess. I've chosen you."

"Me?"

"You. You're perfect."

Perfect. Again, that word. Pauline's mind couldn't handle all this at once. She had to break the information into small morsels.

This robustly handsome, self-possessed, wonderful-smelling man was the eighth Duke of Halford.

Out of all the ladies in this room, he was choosing her, the serving girl.

To be his future duchess.

You're perfect.

Chills raced from the nape of her neck to the soles of her feet, leaving her breathless. Either the whole world had turned on its ear, or after twenty-three years of never being good enough . . . in the eyes of one man—in the eyes of this *duke*—she was perfect.

The duchess cast a cool gaze on her son. "Unnatural child. You live to thwart me."

"I don't know what you mean," he replied calmly. "I'm doing precisely as you asked."

"Be serious."

"I am serious. I've chosen a girl. Here she is." The duke made a sweeping gesture from Pauline's tangled hair to her muddy shoes, painting her with humiliation. "Go on, then. Make her a duchess."

Ah. She understood everything now. She *was* perfect in his eyes. Perfectly dreadful. Perfectly graceless. Perfectly wrong to be a duchess, and by making her an example, the duke meant to teach his interfering mother a lesson.

How clever of him. How obnoxious and insufferable, to boot.

It's your own fault, Pauline. For that one, mad instant, you were a fool.

She didn't find him so handsome anymore. But he still smelled wonderful, drat him.

There was a pause, which no one in the room dared interrupt. It was as though they were spectators to a championship match of some sort, and the duke had just scored a critical point.

Every head swiveled to face the duchess, waiting for her move.

She had no intention of forfeiting. "Well, then. We'll go to the girl's parents."

Brazen strategy, thought Pauline. Two points to you.

"I'd love nothing more." Halford pulled his coat straight. "But I must be returning to Town at once, and I'm certain Simms can't leave her post."

"Certainly I can," Pauline said.

Both the duke and his mother turned to her, clearly irritated that she'd dared interrupt. Never mind that she was subject of their argument.

"I can leave my post anytime." She crossed her arms. "I don't need a post at all, do I? Not if I'm to be a duchess."

The duke gave her a blank look. Obviously, he hadn't expected this reaction. She was probably supposed to stammer and protest and run blushing into the kitchen.

Unlucky for him. He'd picked the wrong girl.

Of course, she knew he'd meant to pick the "wrong girl," but he'd picked the *wrong* "wrong girl." Pauline enjoyed a good laugh as much as the next person, but already she'd lost too much today. She couldn't part with her last tattered remnant of pride.

"Mr. Fosbury," she called in the direction of the kitchen, untying her apron strings. "I'll be leaving now. I don't expect I'll be coming back today. I'm taking this duke 'round to the cottage so he can ask for my hand in marriage."

That brought Fosbury out from the kitchens, looking perplexed as he wiped his floury hands on an apron.

Pauline gave him a reassuring wink. Then she turned to the duchess, smiling wide. "Shall we, your grace?" She made a show of giggling. "Oh, pardon. Did you want I should call you 'Mother'?"

Ripples of hushed laughter moved through the room. The look of aristocratic discomfort on the duchess's face was immensely satisfying.

Whatever stubborn, unfeeling game this duke and his mother were playing, they were gaining a third player in Pauline.

What's more, Pauline was going to win.

Turning her gaze to the duke, she gave him a bold, unashamed inspection. No chore there. The man truly was a fine specimen of masculinity, from broad shoulders to sculpted thighs. If he could ogle her, why couldn't she look right back?

"Cor." She unleashed her broadest country accent as she tipped her head to admire the lower curve of his tight, aristocratic arse. "I'll have great fun with you on the wedding night."

His eyes flared, swift enough to make her insides wince. Could teasing a duke amount to a hanging offense? He certainly possessed the power and means to make her regret it.

But when all the Spindle Cove ladies broke into open, boisterous laughter, Pauline knew it would be fine. She wasn't one of the Spindle Cove set. She was a servant, not a well-bred lady on holiday. But they would stand by her, just the same.

Miss Charlotte Highwood rose and spoke in her defense. "Your graces, we are honored by your visit, but I don't think we could part with Pauline today."

"Then we find ourselves in conflict," the duke said. "Because I don't intend to part with her at all."

The dark resolve in his words sent odd sensations shooting through Pauline. He meant to continue this farce? Stubbornness must run in this duke's family the way green eyes ran in hers.

The duchess tilted her head toward the door. "Well, then. The coach is waiting."

And that was how Pauline Simms, tavern serving girl and farmer's daughter, found herself bringing a duke and his mother home for tea.

Well, and why the deuce not?

If these Quality meant to embarrass her in front of all Spindle Cove, it was only fitting they should sacrifice some pride of their own. She couldn't wait to see the duchess's face when they pulled up before her family's humble cottage. It might do them good to see how common folk lived—to sit on rough-hewn wooden stools and drink from chipped crockery. She and Sally Bright would be laughing over this story for the rest of their lives.

After giving directions to the driver, Pauline joined them

inside the coach. She slid a hand over the calfskin seat, marveling. She'd never touched an actual calf this soft.

She was certain no one of her station had ever been a passenger inside this conveyance, and judging by the grim sets of their jaws, she would guess neither the duke nor the duchess were pleased to have a sugar-dusted serving girl and her muddy shoes joining them now.

Which only made Pauline more resolved—she was going to wring this experience for every last drop of amusement.

For the entirety of the ten-minute drive to her farm cottage, she reveled in inappropriate behavior. She bounced on the seat, testing the springs. She played with the window latch, sliding the glass pane up and down a dozen times.

"What does your father do, Miss Simms?" the duchess asked.

Other than shout, curse, rage, threaten? "He farms, your grace."

"A tenant farmer?"

"No, he owns our land. Some thirty acres."

Of course, thirty acres would be nothing to a true landed gentleman, much less a duke. Halford probably owned a thousand times it.

As the carriage left town, they passed by the Willetts' fields. Mr. Willett's oldest boy was out working in the hops. Pauline put down the window for the thirteenth time, stuck her arm out and waved gaily.

She put her thumb and forefinger in her mouth and whistled loud. "Gerry!" she called. "Gerald Willett, look! It's me, Pauline! I'm going to be a duchess, Ger!"

When she settled back inside the carriage, she caught the duke and his mother exchanging a look. She propped one elbow on the windowsill, covered her mouth with her palm and laughed.

As they neared the cottage, Pauline rapped on the carriage roof to signal the driver. When the coach had rolled to a stop, she reached for the door latch.

"No." With the crook of her parasol handle, the duchess snagged her by the wrist. "We have people for that."

Pauline froze, taken aback. She *was* one of the people for that. Or had the old lady forgotten?

The duke knocked the parasol aside. "For God's sake, Mother. She's not a wayward lamb."

"You chose her. You told me to make her a duchess. Her lessons start now."

Pauline shrugged. If the woman insisted, she would wait and allow the liveried footman to open the door, lower the step, and assist her down with white-gloved hands.

As the duchess alighted, followed by her son, Pauline dipped in a deep, exaggerated curtsy. "Welcome to our humble home, your graces."

She opened the gate and led them through the fenced poultry yard. The gander was after them immediately, honking and ruffling his wings. No one could tell Major he didn't outclass a duke. The duchess tried a freezing look, but quickly resorted to wielding her parasol in defense.

"That'll do, Major." Pauline clapped her hands. Then she ushered her guests inside. "This way, your graces. Don't be bashful. Our home is yours. We're all family now."

The door lintel was low and the duke was tall. He would

have to duck to avoid bashing his head. He paused at the threshold. For a moment Pauline thought he'd simply turn around, return to the carriage, and drive off to London.

But he didn't. He bent at the waist and passed through the doorway in a single, fluid motion.

She had to smile at that. The arrogant duke, literally stooping to enter her family's cottage.

Once inside, the two visitors swept a look around the small, sparsely furnished abode. It wasn't difficult to take in the whole dwelling at a glance. The house was only some dozen paces wide. A stone hearth, a few cupboards, table and chairs. Faded print curtains fluttered in the two front windows. To the side, an open doorway led to the only bedroom. A ladder climbed to the sleeping loft she and Daniela shared.

The rear doorway led to the exterior area where they did all the washing. Soft splashes indicated someone was washing up after the noon meal.

"Mother," she sang out, "look who I brought home from the Bull and Blossom. The ninth Duke of Halstone and his mum."

"Halford," the duchess corrected. "My son is the eighth Duke of Halford. He's also the Marquess of Westmore, the Earl of Ridingham, Viscount Newthorpe, and Lord Hartford-on-Trent."

"Oh. Right. Suppose I should learn it all proper, shouldn't I? I mean, seeing as how it'll be my name, too." She grinned broadly at the duke. "Fancy that."

His lips quirked a fraction. Whether in irritation or amusement, she didn't dare to guess.

"Will you sit?" she asked the duchess.

"I will not."

"If you need the privy," she informed them in a confidential tone, "you go through that door, back around the woodpile, and left at the pigs."

"Pauline?" Mother came through the back door, wiping her hands on a towel.

"Mother, there you are. Has Father gone back to the fields?"

"No," said Amos Simms, darkening the same doorway her mother had just traversed. "No, he 'asn't. Not yet."

She found herself holding her breath as her father peered at the duke, then the duchess.

Lastly, he turned a menacing glare on Pauline.

A sharp tingle of warning volleyed between her shoulder blades. She would pay for this later, no doubt.

"What's all this, then?" her father demanded.

Pauline swept an arm toward her guests. "Father, may I present His Grace, the eighth Duke of Halford, and his mother. As for what they're doing here . . ." She turned to the duke. "I should let his grace explain it."

Oh, excellent. The girl wanted him to explain it.

Griff exhaled, running a hand through his hair. There was no satisfactory explanation he could offer. He had no bloody idea what he was doing in this hovel.

Something sharp jabbed him in the kidney, nudging him forward. That damned parasol again.

Oh, yes. He recalled it now. There was a reason he was

here, and the Reason Herself needed a sharp lesson in minding her own affairs.

He snatched the parasol from his mother's grip and presented it to the farmwife. "Please accept this gift as thanks for your hospitality."

Mrs. Simms was a small woman with stooped shoulders. She looked as faded and wrung out as the dish towel in her red-knuckled hands. The woman stared at the furled parasol, seemingly dumbfounded by its tooled ivory handle.

"I insist." He pressed it toward her.

She took it, reluctantly. "That's v-very kind, your grace."

"Never enter a house empty-handed. My mother taught me that." He shot the duchess a look. "Mother, sit down."

She sniffed. "I don't believe I—"

"Here." With his boot, he hooked a rough wooden bench and pulled it out from the table. Its legs scratched across the straw-strewn dirt floor. "Sit here. You are a guest in this house."

She sat, arranging her voluminous skirts about her. But she didn't try to look pleased about it.

For the next minute or so, Griff learned how it felt to be a menagerie exhibit, as the collected Simms family stood about, gawking at them in silence.

"Mrs. Simms," he finally said, "perhaps you'd be so kind as to offer us some refreshment. I would have a word with your husband."

With evident relief at her dismissal, Mrs. Simms drew her daughter into the kitchen. Griff pulled a cane-backed chair away from the table and sat.

As Simms settled on the other chair, the burly farmer narrowed his eyes. "What can I do for you, yer grace?"

"It's about your daughter."

Simms grunted. "I knew it. What's the girl done now?"

"It's not something she's done. It's what my mother would like her to do."

Simms cut a shrewd glance toward the duchess. "Is her grace needing a scullery maid, then?"

"No. My mother would like a daughter-in-law. She thinks I need a wife. And she claims she can make your girl"—he waved in the direction of the kitchen—"into a duchess."

For a moment the farmer was silent. Then his face split in a gap-toothed grin. He chuckled, in a low, greasy way.

"Pauline," he said. "A duchess."

"I hope you won't be offended, Mr. Simms, if I admit doubts as to the likelihood of her success."

"A duchess." The farmer shook his head and continued chuckling.

The boorish, sinister tone of his laughter had Griff shifting his weight on the chair. To be sure, it was an absurd idea. But even so, shouldn't a man defend his own daughter?

He cleared his throat. "Here's my offer. A man only has one mother, and I've decided to indulge mine. What say I take your daughter to London? There, my mother might have her best crack at transforming her from a serving girl into a lady sufficiently polished and cultured to be a duke's bride."

Simms laughed again.

"Of course, in the much more likely event that this enterprise fails, we will return your daughter to you. At the least, she'll come home with a few new gowns and some exposure to the finer things in life."

"My girl don't need new gowns. Nor any of your finer things."

Just then the girl in question returned to set the table. The dish she placed before Griff was possibly the ugliest teacup he'd ever seen—a cheaply painted bit of china no doubt birthed in some cut-rate factory and passed down through several owners. But before releasing the saucer, she gave it a brisk quarter turn, so that the pathetic, limp flower on the cup would face him and the saucer's chip was on the hidden side.

The meaning in the gesture wasn't lost on Griff. She was a proud one, no question. Also smart-mouthed and bold enough to bait a duke and his dragon of a mother. None of those traits were desirable qualities in a serving girl, much less in a bride.

But they were qualities Griff appreciated in general, and he was beginning to admire this Pauline Simms. Just a bit, and just for herself. During her few minutes in the kitchen, she'd tied back her hair. Her figure remained unremarkable, but now he could see she was more than a little pretty. High cheekbones, gentle nose, eyes tipped at the corners like a cat's. Quite fetching, really, in a rustic, country way. All the farmhands must be mad for her.

You've sworn off women, a voice inside him nagged.

Well, that oath needed some amendment. He'd sworn off *involvement* with women, perhaps. That didn't mean he was going to poke out his eyes. A bit of casual appreciation never hurt anyone—and he suspected it might do this particular woman some good.

"If you're set on her, we can talk." Simms scratched his jaw. "But I can't let her go easy."

Good, Griff thought. No right-thinking father should let a bright, pretty daughter go easily.

The farmer lifted his voice. "Come 'ere, Paul."

She obeyed. As she moved toward them, her mouth was a tight line.

"Look at these 'ands of hers," Simms said, taking his daughter by the wrist and extending her hand and forearm for Griff's inspection.

Her fingers were slender and graceful, but her palm showed the calluses and scars of menial labor—labor more strenuous than serving pots of tea to spinsters. No doubt she helped with the farm work, too.

Simms shook his daughter's wrist, and her hand flopped up and down. "No one else has hands this small. Nor an arm this thin." He made a circle of his thumb and forefinger, easily ringing Pauline's slender wrist. "I've a mare about to foal. Ain't no one else on this farm what can reach up inside and grab the foreleg, if need be."

The farmer slid the ring of his thumb and forefinger from Pauline's wrist all the way to her elbow, visually demonstrating just what equine depths his slender-armed daughter would be called to explore.

Griff's missed breakfast now seemed like a blessing.

"Jes' look at that," Simms said. "She can reach all the way to the womb."

"Father." Pauline snatched her arm away.

"That's worth something, right there," her father said. "Can't let her go without compensation. In advance."

Unbelievable.

Mr. Simms was a farmer. A poor farmer, yes—but not a destitute one. He owned thirty acres. His cottage was humble, but sound. No one was starving under this roof. A strange nobleman entered his home, and he offered, for all intents and purposes, to sell his daughter?

What of the girl's safety? What of her reputation? Griff wasn't the sort of nobleman to buy himself a virgin for despoiling, but Mr. Simms couldn't know that. This was the point where any decent father—hell, any sort of real man— would at least demand assurances. If not tell Griff to take his feudal offer and go straight to the devil.

But Mr. Simms didn't. Which told Griff he was a shoddy excuse for a father and no kind of man at all. The farmer wasn't the least bit concerned about his daughter's health or reputation. No, he just wanted to be compensated in advance. For his extra trouble when the mare foaled.

"This is truly your only objection?" he asked pointedly, giving the farmer a chance to redeem himself.

Mr. Simms frowned. "Not the only objection."

Well, thank God.

"There's the wages she brings home," he continued. "I'll need those in advance, too."

"Her *wages.*"

Griff had the sudden urge to hit something. Something wearing a coarse homespun shirt, dirt-caked boots, and a greedy sneer. That was it. His mother would need to learn her lesson in some other way, at some other time. He needed to leave. This interview either ended now or it ended badly.

Drawing on some generations-old reserve of ducal composure, he rose to his feet. "Perhaps this was an ill-considered plan. The chances of your daughter succeeding in London society are minuscule, and the risks to her are too great." He made his way toward the cottage door, pausing only to catch his mother by the elbow and pull her to her feet. "If you'll excuse me, my mother and I will be on our—"

"Five," the farmer called.

"Excuse me?"

"I'll let her go for five pounds."

Griff could only stare at him. "Good God, man. Are you serious?"

He cracked his neck. "All right, then. You can have her for four pounds, eight. But not a penny less."

Bloody hell. Griff passed a hand over his face. Now he looked as though he was haggling for the girl, determined to ruin her life for the lowest possible price.

"What an excellent bargain." Irony dripped from his mother's words. "I don't think you could find a more economical choice."

"I hope you're happy with yourself," Griff said.

The duchess arched a brow, deflecting all censure back at him. "Are you?"

No. He wasn't. He felt like a first-rate ass. He'd thought himself so damned clever, picking the serving girl out of the spinster crowd. And now he'd invaded her home and forced her to watch while her own father placed a price of four pounds, eight shillings on her health and happiness.

Even for him, this was low.

Miss Simms emerged again, moving toward the table with teapot in hand. Their gazes locked, and her eyes taught him some bold, nameless shade of green. Deep in some unexplored virgin forest, there was a vine of that color, just waiting to be discovered. And there was something essential in this girl's nature that was far, far better than this place.

Just then, Griff observed a telling sequence of events.

A clatter rose from the rear of the house.

With a quiet curse, Pauline Simms stumbled. Hot tea sloshed on the cottage's dirt floor.

"Paul, I told you—" The farmer's hand went up in threat.

And standing four full paces away, Pauline—the girl who would hold her own against a duke—flinched.

He'd seen enough.

"Mother, go ahead to the coach." He quelled her objection with a small gesture, then turned to the girl. "Miss Simms, a word outside. Alone."

CHAPTER THREE

Pauline followed him out the front door and around to the side of the house. The south side, where there were no windows for the family to peer at them. Neither could the duchess view this corner from the carriage. It was just the two of them, alone with a late-blossoming apple tree and the ridiculousness of it all.

She hoped they might have a good laugh and part ways. There would be evening chores to be done before long, and she'd had enough of dukes for one day.

Apparently, he'd reached a breaking point, too. He stalked the yard in long strides. Back, then forth.

"I've reached a decision." He plucked a dead, dangling branch from the apple tree and tapped it on the fence rail. "Simms, you're coming with me to London. This very afternoon."

Her breath left her. "But . . . but why? For what purpose?"

"Duchess training, naturally."

"But you can't truly mean to marry me."

He came to a decisive halt. "Of course I don't mean to marry you."

Well. She was glad they had that settled.

"Let's set a few things straight at the outset," he said. "I might wear fine clothes and possess a splendid carriage, and I've rolled into your life on something that might resemble a whirlwind. Perhaps even a romantic one, to the untutored eye. But this isn't a fairy tale, and anyone who knows me could tell you . . . I am no prince."

She laughed a little. "With all due apologies, your grace, I hadn't formed any opinions to the contrary. I stopped believing in fairy tales long ago."

"Too practical for such things, I suspect."

She nodded. "I'm prepared to work hard for the things I want in life." Sadly, she was still wearing a full year's hard work spattered in her hair and frock.

"Excellent. Because what I'm offering you is employment. I mean to hire you as a sort of companion to my mother. Come to London, submit to her 'duchess training,' and prove a comprehensive catastrophe. Should require little effort on your part."

Pauline's jaw worked but no words came out.

"In exchange for your labors, I will give you one thousand pounds." He leveled his apple-branch switch at the cottage. "And you will never depend on that man again."

One thousand pounds.

"Your grace, I . . ." She didn't even know what to say— whether to call his proposal insufferable, or nonsensical, or a dream come true.

Impossible. That was the best word.

"But I can't. I just can't."

He moved closer. The sun caught amber flecks in his dark brown eyes. "You can. And you will. I will make it so."

She turned her gaze to the cottage, frustrated with his commanding demeanor and his stubbornly enticing scent. He smelled so wretchedly trustworthy.

"Don't worry about your clothes and your things," he said. "Leave it all. You'll have new."

"Your grace . . ."

He tapped the branch against his booted calf. "Don't play at reluctance. What can possibly be keeping you here? A post serving tea to spinsters? Farm labor, and sleeping space in a drafty loft? A brutish father who would eagerly sell you for five pounds?"

She set her teeth. "Five pounds is no paltry sum to folk like us."

And even if it weren't a vast amount, it was five pounds more than "completely worthless," which was how her father set a woman's value most days.

"Be that as it may," he said, "five pounds is considerably less than a thousand. Even a farm girl with no schooling can do that arithmetic."

She shook her head. Amazing. Just when she thought he'd exhausted the ways to insult or demean her, he proved her wrong.

He said, "My mother has too much time at leisure. She needs a protégé to take shopping and drill in diction. I need her diverted from matchmaking. It's a simple solution."

"Simple? You mean to bring me to your home . . . buy me

all new things . . . pay me a thousand pounds. All that, just to cure your mother of meddling?"

He shrugged in confirmation.

"I wouldn't call that simple, your grace. Much easier to just tell her you don't wish to marry. Don't you think?"

His eyes narrowed. "I think you enjoy being difficult. Which makes you the ideal candidate for this post."

Pauline was divided on how to receive that statement. For once, she was someone's ideal. Unfortunately, she was his ideal thorn in the side.

Nevertheless, his offer tempted in a perverse way. For once in her life she wouldn't be failing at success. She'd be succeeding at failure. No more would she hear, "But she *means* well"—the duke didn't want her to mean well at all.

"None of this matters," she said at last. "I can't leave Spindle Cove."

"I'm offering you a lifetime of financial security. All I'm asking in return is a few weeks of impertinence. Think of it as your chance to write the practical girl's fairy tale. Come away to London in my fancy carriage. Have some fine new gowns. Don't change a whit. Don't fall in love with me. At the end of it, we part ways. And you live wealthily ever after." He looked to the carriage. "Just say yes, Simms. We need to be going."

What would it take to convince him? She raised her voice, enunciating each word as best an uneducated farm girl could. "I . Can't. Go."

He matched her volume. "Well, I can't leave you."

The world was suddenly very quiet. The duke went absolutely still. She could have thought him a statue if not for the stray apple blossom decorating his shoulder and the breeze stirring his dark, wavy hair. Somewhere above them a songbird chirped and whistled for a mate.

She swallowed hard. "Why not?"

"I don't know."

He tilted his head and stared at her with fresh concentration. She tried not to blush or fidget as his slow, measured paces brought them toe-to-toe. So close, she could see the individual grains of whiskers dotting his jaw. They were lighter than his hair—almost ginger, in this light.

"There's something about you." His ungloved hand went to her hair, teasing it gently. A little shower of crystals fell to the ground. "Something . . . all over you."

Good heavens. He was touching her—without leave, or any logical reason. And it should have been shocking—but the most surprising part was how natural it felt. So simple and unforced, as though he did this every day.

She wouldn't mind it, Pauline thought. Being touched like this, every day. As though there were something precious and fragile beneath the grit of her life, just waiting to be uncovered.

He dusted more fine white powder from her shoulder. "What *is* this? You're just coated with it."

Her answer came out as a whisper. "It's sugar."

He lifted his thumb to his mouth, absently tasting. His lips twisted in unpleasant surprise.

"Sugar mixed with alum," she amended.

"Oddly fitting." He reached for her again, this time leading with the backs of his fingers.

She felt herself leaning forward, seeking his touch.

"Pauline?" a familiar voice interrupted. "Pauline, who's that man?"

She jumped back and turned to spy Daniela peeking out from the west side of the cottage. After a moment of internal debate, Pauline waved her sister forward. There was no easier way to explain her refusal than to let him see for himself.

"Your grace, may I present my sister, Daniela. Daniela, our guest is a duke. That means you must curtsy and call him 'your grace.'"

Daniela curtsied. "Good day, your grace."

The words came out thick and nearly unintelligible, the way they always did when Daniela was nervous. Her tongue wasn't so nimble with strangers.

"The duke was just leaving."

Daniela curtsied again. "Goodbye, your grace."

Pauline watched him with keen eyes, waiting. People of his rank sent their simple folk to asylums or paid someone to tend them in the attic—anything to hide them from view. Still, he would be able to tell. Everyone could always tell within a minute of meeting Daniela.

The familiar anger welled within her, fast and defensive—a response learned from years of deflecting insults and slights. Her hand reflexively made a fist.

He probably wouldn't resort to name-calling. Idiot, numskull, half-wit, dummy, simpleton. Those words would be beneath a duke, wouldn't they?

But he would have some reaction. They always did. Even well-meaning people found some way to give offense, treating Daniela like a puppy or an infant, instead of like a full-grown woman.

Most likely the duke would curl his lip in disgust. Or turn his gaze and pretend she didn't exist. Perhaps he would sneer or shudder, and that would give Pauline just the surge of anger she needed to send him away.

But he didn't do any of those things.

He spoke in a completely unaffected, matter-of-fact tone. "Miss Daniela. A pleasure."

And as Pauline watched, the duke—God above, a bloody *duke*—lifted her sister's hand to his lips. And kissed it.

Lord help her, for the briefest of instants, Pauline tumbled headlong in love with the man. Never mind his promise of a thousand pounds. He could have had her soul for a shilling.

She briefly closed her eyes, rooting deep in her heart for all those reasons to dislike him. The most petty, stupid one came to her lips. "You didn't kiss *my* hand."

"Of course not." He glanced at the appendage in question. "I know where it's been."

Her cheeks flushed as she recalled her father's "demonstration" in the cottage.

"She is the source of your reluctance, I take it?" he asked.

Pauline nodded. "I can't leave her. And she can't leave home."

After a moment's quiet consideration, he addressed her sister. "Miss Daniela, I want to take your sister to London."

Daniela paled. Her chin began to quiver. The tears were already starting.

"I will bring her back," he said. "You have my word. And a duke never breaks his word."

Pauline raised a brow, skeptical.

He shrugged, conceding the improbable truth of the

statement. "Well, this particular duke won't break this particular word."

"No." Her sister hugged her so tightly, Pauline reeled on her feet. "Don't go. I don't want you to go."

Her heartstrings stretched until they ached. They'd never been apart. Not for even one night. What the duke might describe to her as temporary, Daniela would experience as endless. She'd spend every moment of their separation feeling miserable, abandoned. But at the end of it . . .

One thousand pounds.

They could do anything with a thousand pounds. Escaping their father would only be the beginning. She and Daniela might have a cottage of their own. They could raise chickens and geese, hire a man now and then for the heavy labor. With prudence, the interest alone would be enough to keep them fed and safe.

And she could open her shop.

Her shop. So silly, how she'd come to think of it that way. She might as well have named it Pauline's Unicorn Emporium, as likely as it was to come to pass. It had always been just a dream for someday. But with one thousand pounds, that someday could be quite soon.

"God's knees." The duke's voice intruded on her thoughts. "Not you again."

Major, the old cantankerous gander, had found them once more, and he wasted no time in making the duke feel unwelcome. The bird stretched his neck to its greatest length, puffing his breast in a warlike pose. Then he lowered his beak and made a strike at the duke's boot.

With a crisp thwack, Halford deflected the goose with a

flick of the apple bough. He jabbed the blunt end into the goose's breast, holding the enraged bird at branch's distance. "This bird is possessed by the spirit of a dyspeptic Cossack."

"He doesn't like you," Pauline said. "He's very intelligent."

With a short flight, Major managed to squawk free, and then they were starting all over again. Dueling, duke versus gander.

Halford stood light on his feet, one leg forward and one back, wielding the switch like a foil. "Winged menace. I'll have your liver."

Major cast some aspersions of his own. They were unintelligible to human ears, but no less vehement.

At her side, Daniela ceased to cry and began to giggle.

The tightness in Pauline's chest eased. "Daniela," she said. "Take Major to the poultry yard for me. Then come back."

Her sister spread her arms and shooed the gander toward the rear of the house. Once she was safely out of earshot, Pauline crossed her arms and faced the duke.

"If I agree to this . . ." She willed her voice not to shake. "If I go with you, will you return me home in one week?"

"A *week*?" He tossed the stick aside. "That's unacceptable."

"It's the only way I'll agree. It must be a week. We have a ritual of sorts on Saturdays, Daniela and I. She can understand this. If I promise to be back by next Saturday, she'll know I'm not leaving forever." When he hesitated, she went on, "I assure you, I can prove catastrophic within one week."

"Oh, I don't doubt that." He paused in thought. "A week, then. But we leave at once."

"As soon as I bid my sister farewell."

She turned and looked over her shoulder. Daniela was already on her way back from the henhouse.

"I need a penny," Pauline said. "Quickly, give me a penny."

He fished in his pocket and produced a coin, then dropped it in her outstretched hand.

She peered at it. "This isn't a penny. It's a sovereign."

"I don't have anything smaller."

She rolled her eyes. "Dukes and their problems. I'll be along in a moment."

Pauline drew her sister aside. She pulled her spine straight. The only way to keep Daniela from dissolving was to hold herself together. There could be no cracks in her resolve. She must be strong enough for them both, as always.

"Here's your egg money for this week." She opened Daniela's hand and put the coin in it, closing her fingers over the sovereign before she could notice the color wasn't right. "I want you to go upstairs and put it in the tea tin straightaway. Tomorrow, it goes in the collection at church."

Daniela nodded.

"I'm going with the duke now," Pauline told her. "To London."

"No."

"Yes. But only for a week."

"Don't go. Don't go." The tears streamed down Daniela's reddened cheeks.

Don't cry so, I beg you. I can't bear it.

Pauline very nearly gave in. To distract herself, she thought of the golden coin squeezed in her sister's hand. She imagined a thousand of them, stacked in neat rows. Ten by ten by ten by ten . . .

If only she could explain to Daniela what this would mean for them, and how it would better their lives in all the years to come. But her sister wouldn't want to hear more talk of change. She needed routine, comfort. Familiar tasks to see her through the week.

"I'll be back next Saturday to give you your egg money. I swear it. But you must earn that penny. While I'm gone, you must work hard. You cannot laze abed crying, do you hear? Collect the eggs every day. Help mother with the cooking and the house. When the week's gone, I'll be home. I'll be sitting with you in church next Sunday." She framed Daniela's round face in her hands. "And I will never leave you again."

She hugged her sobbing sister tight and kissed her cheek. "Go inside now."

"No. No, don't go."

There was no good to come of prolonging it. Parting wouldn't get any easier. Pauline released her sister, turned, and walked away. Daniela's sobs followed her as she went through the gate and entered the lane, where the duke's fine carriage waited.

"Pauline?" Her mother's voice, calling from the front step.

"I'll be home in a week, Mum." She didn't dare look back.

When she moved to enter the coach, her step faltered. The duke extended a hand. His hand was ungloved, and when his strong fingers closed over hers, a tremor passed through her.

"Are you well?" he asked. His other hand went to the small of her back, steadying her.

Pauline drew a deep breath. His strong touch made her want to melt against him, seeking comfort. She pushed the temptation away.

"I'm well," she said.

"If you need more time to—"

"I don't."

"Should you go to her?" he asked.

No. No, that would make everything worse.

It was useless to explain. What did it matter if he thought her unfeeling and callous, anyhow? She wasn't after his approval. She was doing this for his money.

"My sister always cries, but she's stronger than you'd think." She released his hand and mounted the stairs on her own power. "So am I."

It took a great deal to impress Griff. Many an afternoon in Court, he'd looked on as officers and dignitaries were awarded ribbons, crosses, knighthoods, and more for service to the Crown. Some likely deserved their honors; many didn't. The pomp and ceremony had him jaded by this point, and God knew he wasn't prone to heroics himself. But he liked to think he could still recognize bravery when he saw it.

He had the feeling he'd witnessed a true act of courage just now. The girl had steel in her. He'd felt it, beneath his palm.

A good thing, too. Because if she was going to spend the next several days with the Duchess of Halford, Pauline Simms was going to need it.

"You have a week," he told his mother, settling into the coach.

"A *week?*" Twin spots of color rose on her cheeks, matching the rubies at her throat.

"A week. Simms's family can't spare her any longer than that."

"I can't possibly accomplish this in a week."

"If our Divine Creator could make the heavens, earth, and all its creatures in six days, I should think you can manage one duchess."

She huffed with indignation. "You know very well I'm not—"

"Wait. Hold that thought." Griff sent a hand into his breast pocket, searching. When he came up empty, he muttered a mild curse and fumbled in his waistcoat pockets, too.

"What on earth are you looking for?" his mother asked.

"A pencil and a scrap of paper. You were about to say you're not God, or something to that effect. I mean to have the exact quote, date, and time recorded. An engraved commemorative plaque will hang in every room of Halford House."

Her lips thinned to a tight line.

"You claimed you could make any woman the toast of London. If you can manage that with Simms in one week, I'll marry her." He leveled a single finger at her. "But if this enterprise of yours fails, you will never harangue me on the subject of marriage again. Not this season. Not this decade. Not this lifetime."

She glowered at him in silence.

Griff smiled, knowing he had her right where he wanted her.

He leaned back, propped one boot on his knee, and stretched his arm across the back of the seat. "If the conditions are unacceptable to you, I can turn this coach around right now."

She didn't object. He didn't turn the coach around.

They forged straight on, and Griff pretended to doze through a lengthy lecture on the vaunted family history. It was a litany of heroes, lawmakers, explorers, scholars . . . All the way from his far-flung ancestors in the Crusades to his father, the great, late diplomat.

Just as the duchess's tale was winding toward the debauched disappointment that was Griff, they paused to change horses and take dinner near Tonbridge.

Thank God.

"This," his mother informed her new charge as they alighted from the carriage, "is one of the finest coaching inns in England. Their private dining rooms are peerless."

Miss Simms made comical shapes with her lips as they entered the establishment. "I should think the Bull and Blossom is the superior place, for my money. More welcoming, and that's certain."

"A duchess does not look for an inn that is welcoming," his mother opined. "A duchess is welcome anywhere, anytime. She relies on the establishment to keep everyone else out."

"Really?" As they were shown into the dining room, Miss Simms turned to the stony footman. "Is that so?"

The footman pulled out a chair, staring forward at the wall.

She gave the blank-faced servant an amused look and waved her hand before his eyes. "Hullo. Anyone home?"

The footman remained still as a wooden nutcracker, until she gave up and sat down.

Griff took his own seat and summoned the waiter with

a look, ordering an assortment of dishes. He was famished.

"Cor," Miss Simms sighed, putting her elbows on the table and propping her chin on one hand. "I'm famished."

The duchess rapped the tabletop.

"What now?" the young woman asked.

"First, remove your elbows from the table."

Miss Simms obeyed, lifting her elbows exactly one inch above the surface of the table.

"Second, mind your tongue. A lady never refers to the state of her internal organs in mixed company. And you will strike *that* word from your vocabulary at once."

"What word?"

"You know the word to which I refer."

"Hm." Dramatically thoughtful, Miss Simms put a fingertip to her lips and cast a glance at the ceiling. "Was it 'famished'? Or 'I'm'?"

"Neither of those."

"Well, I'm confused," she said. "I can't recall saying anything else. I'm just a simple country girl. Overwhelmed by the splendor of this inhospitable establishment. How am I to know what word it is I shouldn't say if your grace will not enlighten me?"

A pause stretched, as they all waited to see whether his mother could be provoked into repeating such a common slang as "cor."

Griff reclined in his chair, happy to wait her out. This was the most enjoyment he could recall at a family dinner.

His mother had been needing someone to manage. She certainly couldn't browbeat *him*—no matter what measures she'd resorted to yesternight—and the servants at Halford

House were too well-trained and stoic. He'd been flirting with the idea of getting her a mischievous terrier, but this was better by far. Miss Simms wouldn't leave any puddles on the carpet.

Perhaps after this week was over, he'd hire his mother another impertinent companion.

But next time he'd find one who wasn't so pretty.

The girl sparkled. *Sparkled*, deuce her. Griff couldn't help staring. Hours of coach travel hadn't dislodged those sugar crystals dusting her form, and his eye couldn't stop searching them out. They were like grains of brilliant sand strewn in her hair, clinging to her skin. Even tangled in her eyelashes.

Worst of all, one tiny crystal had lodged itself just at the corner of her mouth. His awareness of it had long passed distracting and verged on maddening. Surely, he thought, at some point during dinner she would catch it with her tongue and sweep it away.

If not, he'd be tempted to lean forward and tend to the cursed thing himself.

"Miss Simms," his mother said, "if you think you can trick me into repeating your vulgarities, you will be disappointed. Suffice it to say, slang, blasphemy, and cursing have no place in a lady's vocabulary. Much less a duchess's."

"Oh. I see. So your grace never curses."

"I do not."

"Words like cor . . . bollocks . . . damn . . . devil . . . blast . . . bloody hell . . . ." She pronounced the words with relish, warming to her task. "They don't cross a duchess's lips?"

"No."

"Never?"

"Never."

Miss Simms's fair brow creased in thought. "What if a duchess steps on a tack? What if a gust of wind steals a duchess's best powdered wig? Not even then?"

"Not even when an impertinent farm girl provokes a duchess to a simmering rage," she replied evenly. "A duchess might contemplate all manner of cutting remarks and frustrated oaths. But even in the face of extreme annoyance, she stifles any such ejaculations."

"My," Miss Simms said, wide-eyed. "I do hope dukes aren't held to the same standard. Can't be healthy for a man, always stifling his ejaculations."

Griff promptly broke the prohibition against elbows on the table, smothering a burst of laughter with his palm and disguising it as a coughing fit. The violence of it caught him by surprise. He couldn't recall the last time he'd laughed from so deep in his chest that his ribs ached. For that matter, he couldn't recall the last time he'd been tempted to lean across the table and catch a lush, clever mouth in a kiss.

For several months he'd been stifling . . . everything.

"Let it out, your grace. You'll feel better." She looked to him with false concern and a coy, conspiratorial smile.

Oh, he liked this girl. He liked her a great deal.

And that worried him intensely.

About the Author

TESSA DARE is the *New York Times* bestselling, award-winning author of nine historical romance novels and four novellas. A librarian by training and a book-lover at heart, she makes her home in Southern California, where she shares a cozy, cluttered bungalow with her husband, their two children, and a dog.

Visit www.AuthorTracker.com for exclusive information on your favorite HarperCollins authors.